CW01521901

To Vande
With !

November xxxx .

ITALIAN CAPRICE

Peter Rippon

Peter Rippon

Pen Press Publishers Ltd

First published in Great Britain by
Pen Press Publishers Ltd
39-41, North Road
Islington
London N7 9DP

ISBN 1-905203-42-X

Printed and bound in the UK

A catalogue record of this book is available from
the British Library

Cover Illustration by Daniele Ohnheiser

To the memory of my Mother,
herself a consummate story-teller;
who played all the parts and did all the voices.

Epigraph

I consider all men to be my countrymen...
nationality must be subordinate to the universal and
common bond of humanity.

- Michel de Montaigne 1582

Look in my heart, and you shall see
Graved inside of it, 'Italy'.
Such lovers old are I and she,
So it always was, so shall ever be.

- Robert Browning *De Gustibus...*

About The Author

Peter Rippon was born in Birmingham in late 1936 but spent his early life including the War years growing up in Manchester. Recollections of that time include the earthy smell of an Anderson shelter, & an old Shredded Wheat packet full of Dinky toys.

Peter Rippon read Modern Languages and English at Queens' College, Cambridge. He worked in Europe for several years teaching and returned to England in the autumn of 1963 to become a schoolmaster; he retired five years ago. Having brought one career to its conclusion, he is now hoping, in the words of Max Frisch, to entertain older people rather than teach young ones.

Peter Rippon has travelled about Europe from Scandinavia and the Baltic to Greece & the Mediterranean. Favourite haunts are his almost native Lancashire and the North of England generally, Normandy and the Loire Valley, Provence, Italy, Germany especially Berlin, Hamburg and Lubeck where he has friends of long standing from his schoolmastering years who eagerly and loyally await his next novel.

About the Author (continued)

Italian Caprice is his third novel, a 'Grand Tour' tale set in the late eighteenth century which celebrates many of his memories of France, Germany and Italy, and his abiding interest in and love of those countries. Previous titles were *The River Crossing* (1998), an adventure mystery, and *Shadow In Sunlight* (2001), a psychological mystery thriller. He is currently at work upon the story of a young Berliner who in 1825 at the age of twenty left his native city for Paris.

Peter Rippon is a life-long European, one steeped since school-days in the cultures of the continent. He is irredeemably politically incorrect and is married to a wife who shares his love of travel and languages. They have three adult children who have seen far more of the globe than they have.

Amongst his interests are certain selected English and French poets and novelists, music – especially jazz piano, orchestral symphonic, Spanish classical guitar – cosmology, travel, food and wine and, most particularly, conversation, story-telling and the odd whisky and soda in convivial company late at night.

Contents

ITALIAN CAPRICE
Part One

SEBASTIAN HAVERHILL
A Memoir 1885

Sometimes close relationships can contrive one way or another to skip a generation, possibly even two. I knew my grandfather, Sebastian Haverhill, for instance, far more intimately than I ever knew my father, Edward. This was not wholly due to those imperatives of military duty which caused my father to be more frequently absent than home over the first twenty years of my life – before he was eventually killed in his command at Sebastopol, thirty years ago now.

Nor did it have anything much to do with our bearing the same Christian name, my grandfather and I, although the somewhat unusual, *quasi*-continental ring of this may well have contributed a degree of defining idiosyncrasy to unsubtle perceptions. The truth of the matter was in fact much simpler, mundane even; it had to do with an affinity of character, temperament, personalities, and, above all, cast of mind. For, in a family of military lineage reaching back three centuries to the time of the great Elizabeth, my grandfather and I have been, both of us, antiquaries and men of letters, students in their own language of the great German humanists of the last century, of Winckelmann with his love of Greek antiquity, Lessing and the Hamburg theatre, Goethe, truly the *uomo universale* of letters ancient and modern, and Schlegel, with his miraculous translations of Shakespeare. Furthermore, we were not ignorant of the link back to antiquity through the greatness of the Italian Renaissance mind as it manifested itself through painting and architecture. Indeed, one can stand today in the very centre of Berlin and literally *see* the continuity of aesthetic evolution from ancient time right up to our own in the fine buildings of Knobelsdorff and his kind, nurtured in that very matrix, the Italian, of innovation and invention, buildings that, in the midst of this ugly century with its murderous, militaristic obsessions, speak to those who care to listen of altogether finer possibilities.

My grandfather died twenty years ago, at the improbable age of not quite one hundred, but not before he had imparted to me by dint of his example the abiding essence of a deep love of the rationalistic culture of the Enlightenment of the last century – strange anomaly now, in the fetid contemporary climate of both the Evangelical and the Anglo-Catholic's neo-proselytising, so all pervading in their blinkered, paranoid self-righteous conduct. And it was, this love, something to which he would have continued to hold with absolute firmness, rather, one might say, like a pupil of Socrates in the Florence of Savonarola.

And I recall, too, among the many other thoughts that these few bring in their train, that it is one hundred years almost to the very day that my grandfather set out on his Grand Tour of France, Italy and Germany.

In its classical era the Grand Tour had come to be seen as an alternative mode of cultural and intellectual formation, alternative, that is, to the inane deficiencies of the two ancient universities, which had allowed themselves to fall into a shameful, slothful slough of mindless conventionality. What this had amounted to had been no more than on the one hand an arid theologising, and on the other a slavish deference to the more rackety whims of a world of fashion characterised by a posturing, aristocratic self-importance aped by social inferiors. It was the rise of Napoleon – rather than the Revolution in France – that put an end to the old ways that had included the Tour and the values it epitomised. And here the abject capitulation to Napoleon of the Republic of Venice, with all that it had represented – if latterly in somewhat degenerate form – has always seemed to me in some sense to be of central, symbolic significance. In the Royal Naval Museum at Greenwich there hangs a huge, contemporary representation by Sir Charles Eastlake of Napoleon on his way to Saint Helena, standing in that notorious pose of his and glowering moodily out to sea from the quarterdeck of the *Bellerophon*. Somewhere up to the left of him, and slightly in the background, there stands a group of high-ranking officers, their attention quite clearly focussed upon him. They, of course, are the victors, embodying as they do the combined powers of Europe which had brought him low at last after the twenty years of hideous conflict and convulsion which he had inflicted upon the continent in the name of first revolutionary and subsequently French imperial greatness. But what is most striking about the whole composition is the effete refinement of their features contrasted with his, and most particularly the brute energy contained within that stocky, peasant figure. It is as if some swarthy labourer in the fields had momentarily donned the attire of a military commander, and as if, in some strange sense despite the defeated condition of the man, this were the shape of things to come, as if what is implied in the appearance of those onlookers were the demise of an old world on the point of giving way to a newer, more ugly one. Not that the old century had not had its share of strife, in India and the New World - the condition of my own great grandfather at the end of his days had been testimony enough to that – but nevertheless... Militarily, of course, Napoleon had been formidable, on a par with any you might care to name. But if the best he could manage politically was to set himself up as some sort of comic opera imitation of a Roman emperor and make his brothers kings!... Time does, we know, throw up freaks such as this in a way which might strike one as occurring a little too frequently for comfort; many have aped the imperial theme, and no doubt there will be others- if not in my time then almost certainly in the next, the twentieth century. The point in question here, though, is that Napoleon did pull down the supporting pillars of the edifice of eighteenth-century rationalistic civilisation, and what replaced that over Europe at large was an altogether less attractive world, in which emergent states began, after the Congress of Vienna, to jockey for position on the chequerboard of consequence and power. In view of all of which, one cannot but feel on occasion that the Edward Haverhills of this world do occupy a more central place in the scheme of things than the Sebastians, who effectively enjoy the advantages so hard earned by the blood of the Edwards. And I am reminded that Aeschylus himself was more proud of his service in the ranks of the Athenian army than he was of his achievements as a prize-winning dramatist.

The fact remains that I am a Sebastian, and this is to be the tale of my grandfather Sebastian. And so I shall tell it, collating his notes, papers and diaries into a narrative form which may, I hope, impart a kind of coherence more conducive to pleasurable perusal. Although who, other than myself, is ever likely to peruse it I have not even begun to consider.

SEBASTIAN HAVERHILL
1785

From a point on the South Bank of the River Thames, not all that distant from the site of the old Tabard Inn from which Geoffrey Chaucer's pilgrims had set out upon their journey to the great shrine of Saint Thomas-a-Becket at Canterbury very nearly four hundred years previously, a smart private carriage containing three gentlemen was about to depart for Dover and the Channel packet.

One corner of this conveyance was occupied by a young man of bright aspect, dark brown eyes a-glint with intelligence and curiosity; he was attired elegantly if soberly for travel, in clothes already well-worn but of excellent quality and cut. On his knee he held an open volume of Latin verse, the poet Horace on travel and on the Appian Way in particular, with its equivocal boatmen, bad wine and sharp innkeepers. *Minus est gravis Appia tardis- 'The Appian Way is less rough if you take it in stages.'* Sebastian Haverhill, aged twenty, sat and wondered at the moment of his departure upon the Grand Tour of Foreign Parts – for thus he was inclined to think of it – if they would find the Appian Way any different in their time from what it had been in Horace's, and decided that they probably would not. But what a prospect, in any event! Here he was, with his fine Uncle Greenwood and good old Ned Farrell, actually on his way, or almost, to view scenes from Horace, landscapes from Claude and Salvator Rosa as the two latter had painted them. And he would work on his Italian, too, as well as his French and Latin, so that perhaps the next time he took up his Alberti On Painting, *Della Pittura,* he would be able to make rather more of that than hitherto. Sebastian thrilled at the rich prospects about to be opened up to him, and as the carriage began to make its way through the teeming streets of the river bank, past Wren's great Naval College and the Observatory at Greenwich and up the steep gradient in the direction of Blackheath, he sat back and revelled in the good fortune which had brought him to his present state.

For Haverhills, soldiers all but a very few, did not in the usual way of things indulge themselves in adventures of this order. Had it not been for his Aunt Harry... Sebastian smiled to himself at this recollection of a brilliant, irresistible lady some twelve years his senior – one completely at home, it seemed, in the courts and principalities of Italy and the châteaux of France – who had taken a very much less than proper interest in her handsome young nephew and had taught him a great deal that had redounded to their mutual delight. Darling, adorable Harry! He recalled the breathless, rumpled circumstances in which he had gasped out those words the last time... And decided that a *quasi* public place such as this was not for entertaining thoughts of so disquieting a kind as might easily become embarrassingly obvious. Sebastian adjusted the angle of his Horace slightly where it lay in his lap. Aunt Harry it had been, the incomparable Mrs de Savigny, who for whatever reasons of her own had persuaded her brother Simon, sadly much diminished and debilitated by his service of the previous decade against the rebellious colonials of the American dependency, now alas the United States, that the boy must certainly do the Tour.

So, the boy was embarking upon the Tour. And he confidently expected to be able to rendezvous with his wicked aunt, as she had intimated they might, in, of all places, *Venice!* Harry, with the odour of the cigar they had shared upon her breath, and the *chèvrefeuille* scent of Provecnal honeysuckle in the marvellous cleft between her breasts. At Carnival time, in due course... Cocooned in the memory of erotic delight and invigorated by the prospect of more to come, Sebastian sat back in his seat , at one with his destiny.

Next to him there sat an old friend – if friendships at the age of twenty can be said to be old – a boon companion in such vital matters as fist-fighting, sword-play and tennis, one Edward Farrell, the 'Honourable Ned', only son of a noble earl of fabulous wealth whose solution to the problem of the boy's inept and rackety goings-on over dogs, horses, cards and women of a decidedly equivocal kind, was to pack the lad off abroad for a while, to see if it did him any good, or whatever. Not that he could bring the family name into any greater disrepute than he, Lord Withybrook himself, had done, but for one so young the boy had already shown himself to be somewhat too inclined to make free, very free with the family fortunes and had begun to make unacceptable inroads... Effectively the project was about getting rid of him, and most urgently and particularly after the Honourable Ned's latest escapade with the Penge Mangler from which, after some ten rounds spiritedly and courageously fought, he had been fortunate indeed to come off still alive and in one piece and still relatively sane, if the notion of sanity was one to be entertained where Ned was concerned. Not that the episode had done him too much harm with his father's club cronies, for at White's bets had been laid.

"Spirited lad, that boy of yours, Withybrook. Takin' on the Mangler, eh? Heard about it from a man I know."

Lord Withybrook had shuddered; he too knew the man of whom his friend had spoken. Timothy Kydd, of Stepney. A cockney opportunist of a type known since time immemorial, one who most profitably serviced the interests of rich men young and old with little sense and the fortunes to indulge their lack of it. Cock-fights, dog-fights, encounters of the pugilistic variety and others involving girls usually of the less hygienic kind - although the tentacles of Kydd did extend even into the more exalted reaches of social life, and he could invariably manage a spot of high-class trade too, at a price – Tim Kydd was a fixer *par excellence* where all of these were concerned, a master of whores and all kinds of other, less flavoursome ancillaries and agents. He was a man who could make himself of much use to those in need, and equally not a man to cross, given the naked power he commanded by virtue of sheer terror right across the more *louche* haunts of the metropolis.

So Ned had been packed off with Sebastian.

"You can go with that school-friend of yours, the one I once saw do you over at the foils. Gentlemanly, stylish sort of fellow. Good connections too, I gather. I'll have a word with his people." And the noble earl, probably not without ulterior and lecherous motive however merely wishful, had made his approach to Colonel Haverhill through Mrs de Savigny, and the things had been fixed accordingly.

The third member of the travelling party was of a very different order from both young men. Julian Greenwood, Esquire, an older kinsman of Sebastian on his mother's Fairfax side. An independent gentleman from the North of England, and one of philosophic and literary inclinations, already much travelled and adept at the major languages of France, Germany and Italy, this was the mentor, the guide, tutor and guardian. Cajoled into the project, albeit without much need of persuasion at the prospect of adventurous enterprise, Julian belonged to a branch of the Greenwoods connected by marriage with Sebastian's mother's family, a branch which the Colonel in his obstinate, pernickety way persisted in seeing as having 'questionable' links with recusant Lancashire Catholicism. But Harriet, in characteristic style, had wasted little time in over-riding her brother's hesitations.

"Nonsense, Simon. Fiddlesticks! Mr Greenwood is a respectable, scholarly gentleman and one who, I may remind you, is highly regarded amongst the *literati* of the metropolis and others in fashionable *and* political circles. Why, he dines at Devonshire House, man! Would you prefer to hire a common or garden bear-leader? Some clammy cleric from one of the universities? I just know Sebastian and Julian will do very well together, and what is more, some of their interest in things may even work its effect upon Withybrook's boy, whatever his name is."

"You know perfectly well what his name is, Harriet. Do not play games with me."

But the Colonel's protest had been no more than a gesture. Once Harriet got the bit between her teeth...But then, she did know the world, and in a way Catherine, his wife, would never wish to.

"Julian knows the world, Simon. He is perfectly at home in Berlin, Paris, Rome or Venice. He has connections, influence; his name carries weight in artistic and diplomatic circles wherever it is known. Yes, Simon, known, *and* highly regarded. One simply could not do better."

The Colonel had wilted privately at her mention of *milieux* he preferred to know as little of as possible, spheres peopled by men – and women, too – whose thoughts were never quite what they seemed to be, never quite what their words appeared to suggest. But the thing was under way, and since it had begun to seem rather unlikely that Sebastian would fulfil his father's dearest wish and take the King's commission and march with the colours, then this might well be the best way forward. Though why people should wish to put themselves to such expense and inconvenience to leave home and consort with strangers abroad the Colonel found it hard to imagine. The fact remained that people like Harriet and Greenwood – perfectly genteel and reputable people, he had to allow – seemed to be at it all the time, and to thrive on it. For Harriet certainly throve. Of that there could be no doubt. So be it then, he concluded. God bless the boy. God bless my dear son, and let him take his chance where he may.

Simon Haverhill sat in his den, a library full of books he had never even opened, and pondered with some regret. Had I only been up to it, to school the boy in military affairs... But he had to acknowledge, with a soldier's realism, that this was no more than wishful thinking on his part. Sebastian must find his own way, if the career of arms was not for him.

*

From his place in the carriage Julian surveyed the two boys opposite him. An unlikely pair they made, and his whimsical spirit delighted in the incongruity of the friendship between two so disparate young men. There was Sebastian, a devilish handsome, elegant fellow if ever there was one, with his thick, wavy chestnut hair and large, lively brown eyes, perfectly if modestly tailored – no doubt by Simon's London man - slender, lithe, youthful, but at the same time understated, unobtrusive, gentlemanly- a credit to his family and in particular to that father of his, if a military idiot like Simon could be allowed any credit in the matter; an unlikely son of his Fairfax cousin Catherine and her much diminished husband, Julian mused. But then, who could ever tell, in these matters? Certainly Simon had had a hard time in the American colonies, and his spirit had been perhaps unduly afflicted, no doubt in consequence of wounds sustained in action and their debilitating effect on the moral fibre of the man. He had returned, Colonel Simon Haverhill, in the aftermath of that disastrous enterprise to which the former colonists were now referring as their 'War of Independence', in very poor condition and had simply never recovered the energy of a man in ordinary, rude health, something which tended to be taken for granted among those of their class brought up to ride, to exercise at fence, to lead active, country lives. And it was after all the price not infrequently paid by the professional soldier for his duty and his service to his sovereign. Usually unacknowledged. The halt, the lamed, the mutilated and the otherwise impaired did not appear at the customary rituals of thanksgiving for Victory in the cathedrals of the land. Fortunately though, the Haverhills were not dependent upon the bounty of the King, given their private circumstances. Simon was no wretched cast-off, flung aside on half-pay and left to make out as best he might. But he should take a pride in his fine son, soldier or no, and he, Julian Greenwood, was to see to it that Sebastian was exposed to the finest and most edifying influences the ancient civilisations of the continent could provide. Somewhat to his surprise, he found himself rather looking forward to his function as mentor and guide to the responsive pupil he already knew Sebastian to be, with his eager, good-humoured interest in languages, architecture and painting. As for the other one...

Julian turned his attention to the Honourable Ned. Had it not been for the private communication he had received in his Lancashire manor from the Foreign Secretary concerning the present state of the French nation and the need for a trustworthy agent to take a close look on the ground as it were, not even Harriet's wiles could have prevailed upon him to contemplate the best part of two years to be spent in the company of such a young man. But Greenwoods were nothing if not trustworthy, and had been indeed since the days of Francis Walsingham himself, first Intelligencer to the great Elizabeth, and the man who in his day, as Greenwood legend had it, would have known of every visit to the privy made by Philip of Spain in the very depths of the impregnable Escorial fortress-palace itself.

Huge blue eyes, slightly bulging, probably not much mind in there, Julian thought, although one must not prejudge the matter, in fairness to the boy. Hair so fair as to be almost white, at the moment sticking out untidily from beneath a tricorne travelling hat, the Honourable Ned, muscular and of great strength, seemed to bulge ungainly out of his clothing, as *délabré* as he himself and Sebastian were *soigné*. Certainly not much effort or care had been taken over his tailoring. Could the noble Earl of Withybrook have been so unconcerned about how his heir presented himself to the world? Julian's decidedly tangential acquaintance with that unappetising specimen of aristocracy told him that it was more than likely that the father simply did not possess the *nous* even to consider the matter for an instant.

Julian had not been at all pleased to begin with, at the proposed addition of this youth with his reputation for this and that, even if he was Sebastian's good friend. Not that it was the fact of it that troubled him all that much, but rather the manner. But one should begin by allowing the benefit of the doubt before rushing to judgment, and one might perhaps endeavour to persuade the young man that a little *finesse* in his affairs of whatever kind could go a very long way with his parent- that he, Edward, could have a far better time all round and in every senseif he would only take pains to eschew notoriety. Not without a touch of cynicism which he readily and gleefully acknowledged, Julian decided that an appeal to self-interest would probably be the line of approach most likely to succeed, although there just might have to be an exchange of views, a trial of conclusions even, first. But if so, so be it.

Damn Harriet for her persuasiveness, adorable as she was, and damn political contingency for what it had that made convenient cover of a journey such as this upon which they were now embarking. And Julian allowed himself to wonder, not too seriously, just what kind of accommodation had been arrived at between his irresistible lady cousin and that repulsive old satyr, Withybrook. No doubt some kind of material advantage had been engineered from the need of the noble earl, since Harriet's capacity for expenditure was simply enormous, and Peter de Savigny, estranged from his lady wife, had become all too cavalier in his provision. It was known as more than rumour that he had gambled away a huge fortune around the gaming houses of London, Paris and elsewhere, and that his father, Lord Hawkhurst, had disinherited him utterly, so that the title and estate must now either skip a generation or devolve sideways. Harriet and Peter were rarely seen together now, and it had begun to look as if the production of a male heir in the Hawkhurst line could well be at risk. Something decidedly peculiar there; odd indeed, with so vast a fortune at stake and Harriet's avid interest in both riches and position. Surely, Julian surmised, she was not one to allow things to remain as they were. Harriet would be about it, one way or another.

The carriage had successfully negotiated the pull up the hill from Greenwich and was now making its way easily across Blackheath. Julian Greenwood allowed his thoughts to turn from the boys and Harriet to Lord Temple's letter, in view of which Harriet's importunity, castigated as such by himself and dismissed equally peremptorily by that lady, had in fact proved mightily fortuitous. For traditionally Greenwoods did not seek office in public life but awaited the call which they knew would come sooner or later. And much as he loved the unassuming but to him incomparable manor house up by the Forest of Bowland and the rain-swept moorland of North Lancashire, not to mention the clubs and coffee-houses and theatres of a capital city, London, without compare anywhere in the world known to him, Julian felt his spirits rise, both at the call from the Foreign Secretary and at the prospects extending before him and his charges on those travels which were just beginning. And he found himself hoping with all his heart that the boys' sense of thrill and adventure would come to match his own which, over all the years, had yet to fail him.

Edward spoke as if on cue.

"Sir?"

"Yes, Mr Farrell?"

"Do you imagine that, at Paris, there might be a chance of a visit to Maître Courtois?"

"The fencing master? Most certainly, sir. I have already written to him."

"You... know him, sir?"

"I do."

"And you've... fought with him?"

"He has instructed me, yes."

"At considerable length, and in all weapons. So, Farrell, what I would advise is... a degree of caution." The Honourable Ned ignored his friend and plunged on.

"Sir?"

"If this is not an impertinence, do you think we might try a pass or two, sometime?" Julian warmed to the awkward young man opposite him.

"I shall be delighted, sir. Absolutely delighted." Sebastian snorted.

"Ned- oh, well..." The tone of this, quite deliberately, conveyed an amused resignation; it was designed to provoke, and it did just that.

"Oh well what, man?"

"Nothing at all. Time, old fellow, Time will tell."

"At Courtois', then, sir?"

"Chez Courtois, mon cher Monsieur."

Was it Julian's few words of French, perhaps, that so vividly brought home to all three of them something of the reality of the enterprise to which they had so recently committed themselves? As it was, the three exchanged happy grins of complicity, as fellow initiates, practitioners of a mystery will do, and sat back in warm anticipation of sport to be had.

"I am thinking, sir, that we shall need some unstiffening after this journey if we are to do ourselves justice in the *salle d'armes,"* said Sebastian.

"Most certainly we shall, my boy. Most certainly. One does not go cold to Maître Courtois."

"Some tennis first, then, perhaps," suggested Edward, "Amongst other things."

"The very thing, sir. The very thing."

Julian was pleased; the spirit of the undertaking had begun to take hold, thanks to Mr Farrell's mention of the famous fencing master, coach and instructor to countless gentlemen from England, France, Germany and even more northerly regions. Any swordsman worth his blade would recognise the style of Courtois the instant he observed it. A former French Army officer of impoverished minor nobility who had served with Montcalm in his time, Thibault Courtois de la Motte du

Hêtre had set up his *salle d'armes* in the Marais, just off the Rue des Francs Bourgeois, after leaving the service, and had rapidly acquired both fame and prosperity- albeit in terms of earned money – by virtue of a *quasi*-magical understanding and command of the science of fence. Julian wondered if the boys appreciated how very fortunate they were that he had been able to claim special privilege with the famous Master and decided they probably had not the faintest idea. But he saw that his stock had risen with Edward Farrell, and was wryly thankful that it was a matter of sword-play that was in question, and not fisticuffs.

The carriage rolled steadily forward, out into Kent and on down the immemorial route to Dover and the Channel. How many countless mounted riders bearing crucial intelligence – military, commercial, political – had plied this highway? Lithe young Roman officers, hard as nails and fighting fit; Norman knights of similar ilk; Lombard Bankers, subtle in negotiation and possessed of several languages; Elizabethan merchant adventurers... It was getting on for two thousand years now, by and large, and would no doubt continue far into the future. Julian simply could not imagine any end to it all; as long as men's affairs required the swift exchange of information, mounted riders would ply the thoroughfares of Europe. He turned his thoughts to the content of the Latin text Sebastian had before him, particularly and with some amusement to his recollection of Horace's account of dreadful wine and cheating inn-keepers along the Appian Way, as the poet kept company with his Greek friend Heliodorus, *rhetor comes Heliodorus/ Graecorum longe doctissimus...* by far the best Greek rhetorician alive. None of that would have changed since the last time he had travelled that route, either. But nothing could mar the thrill of the traveller's sense of unfamiliar vistas about to open up, or even old favourites due to open up again. The sounds of French being spoken around one, the alien tastes of food grown and cooked differently, the aroma of different tobacco... truly, the man who tires of all this, or allows himself to become indifferent to it is decidedly the poorer in consequence.

They put up that night, by previous arrangement, at the Bell at Bromley, where they all three ate a hearty dinner before savouring a respectable claret.

"My Father, sir, drinks nothing but French wine. He would maintain that such others as exist are simply not for gentlemen."

"Then I have to say, Edward, that I am of a different opinion; and as we travel, sir, you shall sample not only the best of the French vintages, but the German wines from the rivers of Moselle and Rhine, the Italians from the northern lakes and the vineyards of Piedmont and Tuscany. Names such as Barbera and Barolo shall ring in your ears, Bardolino, Chianti, Valpolicella, Montepulciano d'Abruzzo and many others. Then at least you shall know of these, even if you eventually reject them." How could old Withybrook be such an ass? And a pompous one at that. Julian could picture him, holding forth to cronies in all his self-regard, self-importance. And if the son parroted such a father, what else might one expect the lad to get up to? Julian had the sense that he had taken on not just the pugilist, but the whole awful edifice of prejudice and preconception inherited from one not renowned for wisdom. A voice echoed in his memory, that of the Foreign Secretary in the recently elected Pitt administration, Lord Temple.

"I understand you are travelling with young Haverhill and that Farrell boy. Awful old fool, Withybrook, you know, Greenwood, and the lad's probably no better. How could he be, God help him, with a sire like that? But, good cover, this Grand Tour thing, wouldn't you say? Yes, good cover."

Julian had made some non-committal reply to the Foreign Secretary, who was far too well-acquainted with his circle of friends, relatives and others to be prevaricated with anyway. But at least the boy, in his inept way, had made an attempt at conversation. Julian, himself unmarried and childless, began to warm to him; he was worth more than his father had allowed, and his efforts should be acknowledged, his thoughts coaxed into larger perspectives.

"Sir?"

"Sebastian?"

"You are familiar with the Roman writers, are you not?"

"I am."

"Would you know, then, whether the wines mentioned in Latin texts actually still exist? Whether under the old names, or more recent ones?"

"Do you know, Sebastian, I am unable to answer that. You disconcert me, sir. But we might remember to find out, don't you think?"

"We might remember to try 'em, too," said the Honourable Ned.

"Certainly, Edward," said Julian, "certainly we shall. But there are other things worth your anticipation too, gentlemen, if I may put it thus. For instance, I cannot begin to tell you what an impression your first sight of Italy will make upon you as we come over the Alps and enter that country. The painters never really contrive to capture the spirit of the place, not entirely. Although I can quite see how the term 'picturesque' may quite naturally have come into being. Does the name William Gilpin mean anything to you, Sebastian? Or to you, Edward?"

"No, sir."

"Nor to me, sir."

"An acquaintance of your Aunt Harriet, I understand, Sebastian, who takes an interest in these matters. He studies 'the picturesque', that which is *'pittoresco',* that is, worth painting . No doubt he will produce a treatise, or something similar, on the subject sooner or later."

"Not my style, sir. Wine and swordplay more in my line."

"Ah, but tomorrow, Ned, you shall look through my Claude glass. Then we'll see."

"Your what, man?"

"Do you have one about you, Sebastian?"

"I do, sir. Aunt Harriet found it somewhere and insisted I take it. Most intriguing. I shall definitely try it out on Mr Farrell."

"And just what, exactly, will you 'try out' on me?"

"You shall see, old fellow. Tomorrow, or perhaps when we reach France."

*

That evening Sebastian began the diary it was his intention to keep for the whole of the Tour.

I find it hard to believe, he wrote, *that we are at last on our way, having set out, as have so many others before us, from the South Bank of the Thames down the historic highway to Dover, from whence we shall effect our crossing of the Channel to France, the first stage of our progress into the mainland of the continent – to Paris, then on to the Loire where, it is said, the best French is spoken, and eventually on again down to Provence from whence we traverse the mighty Alpine range of mountains into, at last, Italy – to the great lakes of the north, then Florence, Sienna, Rome, Naples, Venice ... Our return northwards is planned to take us into the German-speaking lands and up to Berlin, for which, it seems to me , my Uncle Greenwood has a special affection – not that he does not somehow exude a quiet delight in our undertaking, our 'adventure' at large, rather in the style of certain officers of my father's acquaintance who I recall.*

Beside me in the carriage, a berlin so generously put at our disposal by Grand-mama Fairfax, sits old Ned Farrell, bursting with energy as always, but strangely – to me at least – unaffected by the prospect of the tremendous vistas, unfamiliar sights and novel experiences which lie in wait for us over the water. But he and I shall keep each other in trim, at the jeu de paume, *once we have found it, and in the* salle d'armes. *And a propos, mention has already been made of Maître Courtois – a legendary figure indeed, and we are to receive instruction from him! One might have known, of course, that my Uncle Greenwood would number him amongst his acquaintances, that he too would have exercised at the famous salle d'armes in the Rue des Francs Bourgeois; but to hear him offer a pass or two at the foils or whatever to Ned – that really did bring home all the marvellous actuality of this moment in a way the previous weeks of laborious preparation had not done. He sits there, my Uncle Greenwood, in the carriage, perfectly composed, self-possessed, gentlemanly – and I could wish on this score that Farrell were not quite so damnably self-conscious about rank, it really is not quite the thing – a connection to be truly proud of. He will make a splendid guide and mentor on this two-year adventure, and I am resolved to profit to the utmost from his familiarity with the languages of France and Italy, not to mention the German – if only for the lack of time to apply oneself to that in addition. For I do find the idea of that tongue an intriguing one, despite the conventional view and despite the fact, as I understand it, that the gentlefolk of those lands in which it is spoken conduct their lives in the French. Then, to return to my Uncle Greenwood, there is his Latin, and his swordsmanship. Decidedly, there is much to this connection, and much to this particular Greenwood, and it is more than my Aunt Harriet was able or willing to convey. One always knew of him, of course, the Esquire of that northerly manor up by the Forest of Bowland; I do recall even the briefest of visits there, with Father some years ago. But the unassuming ease of his manner in town, the familiarity of his sense of metropolitan ways, the extent of his acquaintance both here and abroad do put a rather intriguing complexion upon the matter of this Lancashire kinsman of my mother, the Greenwood nephew of Grandmama Fairfax. One is left unequivocally with the impression that there is more, much more to Mr Greenwood than meets the eye ...*

However all that may be, a modicum of Bowles now, to round off a memorable day. How Harry comes to be acquainted with these obscure literary figures I should dearly love to fathom. And one should savour such a poet, for it is not merely the great names in the annals that should be cherished. The Reverend William on the picturesque should do very well; perhaps one day he will publish his little collection.

Tomorrow we continue our journey in the direction of Canterbury; then, subsequently, Dover. For this is the time-honoured route to the continent of Europe; one begins to savour ones place in a continuity that stretches back to the days of Rome, and with this sense there comes the awareness that Latin texts will take on a new, contemporaneous significance, since so little has changed over the intervening time where travel is concerned. Truly, a kind of magic begins to come into play, even if we are only at the end of our very first day out. But this will require further examination, for to dismiss the process as mere 'magic' is to find far too simple an answer to what is in question. Does Mr Gibbon have anything on this, I wonder, in his Memoir? Or is he too hag-ridden by the sense of his own superiority to have considered the matter? I shall endeavour to ascertain what I may of this. For my private interest, of course. For it would ill become me to speak disparagingly of one whose achievements have been so rightly acclaimed.

And so, duly, they came to Dover, where the Channel awaited them, and delayed them for the best part of two days, given the fearsome unpredictability of its moods.

*

"God damn it! Begging your pardon, sir," said the Honourable

Ned, pacing the morning room of the inn like a caged lion. "When will it make an end, this weather?"

The young man shadow-boxed himself against the wall then turned, as though at bay.

"Presumptuous youth," said Sebastian, as deliberately casual and off-hand as he could contrive, "thinkest thou to command the elements?"

"*What?*" "You can't do anything about it, can you? So contain yourself Nedward, old cully."

"Old *what?*"

"Old cully. Old friend. A glimpse of the sea usually brings to mind the language of the lower deck, I find. Sailors and things, jack tars. Does it not with you?"

"Grrr!"

"Precisely."

"Edward," said Mr Greenwood from behind his broadsheet by the fire, "I have it here that two practitioners of the noble art –of fisticuffs, that is– fought one another to a standstill over fifteen rounds the other day. The Tottenham Tiger and...the Penge Mangler."

"Oh, good old Sid! I knew I should have laid a bet."

"*Who,* Farrell?"

"Sid Venus, the Penge Mangler. And bully for him!"

"But, he nearly killed you!"

"Well, that is rather the point, ain't it?"

From behind his broadsheet Julian Greenwood noted the understatement and smiled to himself. Decidedly, there was more to this young man than he had been led to believe.

"But, what could it have been like, facing a man like that?"

Edward paced the length of the pleasant room, with its bay-window looking out onto a harbour at present lashed with rain.

"I will tell you precisely what it was like," he said, then paused. In the background the rustle of newsprint paper was audible, as Julian Greenwood stopped reading to listen.

"Go on, man," said Sebastian, but in a tone of quiet

encouragement rather than of the mock derision which the friends so frequently used to one another.

"It was like... Coming face to face with the Devil Himself," said Ned. "I was petrified, to begin with; I very nearly lost control of my insides, if you will forgive me, sir. Then I realised that whatever it was that the old Mangler was doing to make me feel like that, he was doing it deliberately as part of his fighting technique. So I stopped being afraid and just fought him, blow for blow. Because, if you are afraid, in a fight, you lose. Anyone will tell you that. So, you simply cannot afford to be."

"But why take it on in the first place?" asked Sebastian, "I could not imagine doing a thing like that, ever."

"Just as well," said Edward with relish, "because you would not have lasted fifteen seconds, believe me."

"I do believe you. But you have not answered my question. Why do it in the first place?"

"I did it," said Edward slowly, "for regard, and because I wanted to see if I could. I had fought with all manner of men of my own age and class at school, and so on. You remember, Sebastian?"

"I do."

"I wanted, just this once, to try conclusions with a real pugilist. And at the end of the bout, when the Mangler came over to shake hands he said, 'I shall remember you, young gentleman.' I honour him for that, as the equal of any man in the land."

"Bravo, Edward," said Mr Greenwood, comfortably at ease in his armchair, swathed in aromas of rich roast coffee, newsprint and cheerfully blazing logs. Somehow, Sebastian had the impression, his Uncle contrived to suggest the convivial male comforts of the club-room or the coffee house. "Bravo, by God. Do you know, sir, all sorts of men at my club made all sorts of money on you?"

"By betting I might just last more than a round or two, I suppose? So did cronies of my Father's, at White's. Where are you, sir?"

"Brooks's", said Julian, and was amused to note from the boy's reaction that he had passed this rather obvious test of social status with flying colours.

"Gentlemen," said Sebastian from the bay-window, "it seems to be brightening up out there. And the sun is coming out."

HARRIET DE SAVIGNY
1785

Harriet de Savigny sat at her desk and gazed out at the trim parkland of her Father-in-Law's Sussex estate. Here, at a significant distance from town, she was as always swathed in folds of loving concern by the kind of old earl and his sweet countess. Charlotte, her four-year old daughter, was taken off her hands by a nursery staff of devoted retainers ably managed by the child's grandmother; she, Harriet, was cosseted with fine cuts of meat and succulent fowl, the best wine, favourite puddings.

She was not unaware, of course, despite her affection for the elderly couple who had so generously welcomed her into the family circle, that there was something in addition to spontaneous human warmth, precious as this was, to their solicitude. The whole business hinged upon the question of inheritance and the production of a male heir to the Hawkhurst title and estate in the next generation, her husband, Peter, having been finally denied the succession by his father in view of the wayward racketings which had brought him into dishonour and close even to worse, if there could be said to be worse. Harriet, a child of military lineage, rather doubted if there were; in her family you died facing the enemy. By that as it may, Peter de Savigny, once a fine and handsome figure, had some ten years previously captured the heart of the elegant if little known Miss Haverhill and swept her away on a wave of fashionable approbation – to the goatish envy of most of his metropolitan friends and club land acquaintances.

"Lucky young dog, Savigny! Egad, man, have you seen the lady?"

This had been the point at which gentlemen would leave the matter, in explicit terms at least, although everyone knew quite specifically what was in question. For there was something of perfection in Harriet - in the way in which she was made and the obvious purpose of that, as well as in the vital intelligence of her mind and the vivacious warmth of her. In later life she would become imperious, accustomed to command by force of will and a mind which moved faster than most, as well as by sexual blandishment, but that time was not yet. Meanwhile, men recognised in her – and frequently perhaps without quite understanding what it was they had perceived – something of the timeless character of the great courtesan, the kindness, the high spirits and the unequivocally erotic element in all this. What Harriet epitomised was a categorical, pèremptory denial of all that is kill-joy in the human condition; what she asserted was the essential rightness of a certain specific kind of hedonism in furthering the continuance of humankind.

What her husband represented was excess beyond control; Peter de Savigny, dissolute to the core and 'as corrupt as they come' soon tired of the delights of his magnificent lady and went rollicking back to his old haunts and practices. For he was, it seemed, a man on whom all the persuasions of good sense and virtue were completely lost when weighed against the addictive power of traditional vice – wine, cards and the kind of women who at a price would tolerate the effete fumblings of the dribbling drunkard.

So Harriet, great now with Charlotte, was left to her private occasions, effectively abandoned, foisted on to his family at Hawkhurst Savigny. But the feckless dereliction of the man had left her with an appalling dilemma. For, while she genuinely loved the Hawkhursts her in-laws, the noble old earl and his countess, she was fully aware that they were hoping against all probability that Peter would sooner or later do what in duty was paramount and sire a son and heir upon Harriet. Which she was equally determined he should not. So, there would have to be some kind of alternative solution to this *impasse*, and one that ideally should gratify them in one way, her in quite another, and Peter not at all. She therefore had it in mind to contrive a situation in which Peter should, ironically, be seen to enjoy the status of fatherhood in full awareness that his position was totally false; and in the interest of the Hawkhurst inheritance he should writhe in that knowledge for the rest of his mean, miserable life. Revenge, as the Italians have it, is a dish best eaten cold, and Harriet's sense of the aesthetic of the matter fell in quite naturally with that style of design.

So, the elegant Mrs de Savigny made her return to the fashionable world of the metropolis, where she found it much easier to carve out her niche than it could ever have been in her earlier reign as Miss Haverhill. She set out to make friends among the influential and the politic, to extend her acquaintance abroad, to Paris and beyond, and entered into a brief, idyllic love-affair with an Italian prince, largely conducted in a discreet villa in the hills above Torri del Benaco on Lake Garda.

Prince Fabrizio di Benaco, some ten years older than Harriet, had been a wise, expert lover steeped in the ancient lore of the erotic, and although the time was not appropriate for the implementation of the plan which had already outlined itself in her mind, and although the affair soon ran its affectionate and grateful course, it did leave Harriet with a completely novel and revelatory sense and appreciation of the technical possibilities of love-making, a matter-of-fact knowledge of what previously she had only surmised and never experienced. Her debt to Fabrizio, she understood, was beyond estimation – she had taken to his advances with a natural enthusiasm and enjoyment which is granted only to the truly fortunate in this life, and happily she was by now assured enough in mind and imagination to benefit from it all to a degree that rendered her even more magically radiant than she had been in her virginal youth.

Harriet de Savigny returned to London that autumn to take her place and effortlessly to hold her own in the most glittering circles of fashionable society, where gentlemen quizzed the lady and gasped in admiration at what they saw – or sensed – about her. But their gasps of admiration were not without some apprehension, and thus Harriet trod elegantly and with caution through the minefield that is the life of metropolitan society. To the excellent French that she had worked so hard since childhood to acquire, she now, in the aftermath of Fabrizio, added Italian- always an accomplishment. She was, equally, assiduous in cultivating her friendships, even as, frequently and quite without effort or design in these instances, she found herself the object of the most affectionate regard on the part on many of her urban acquaintances.

At the moment Harriet was engaged in communication with just such a friend, now exiled – as she herself saw it – for reasons of health to the South of France, where she languished in an improbably beautiful family villa built in the style of Renaissance Tuscany high above the Mediterranean, which it overlooked, somewhat to the west of the frontier with the Italian kingdom of Piedmont.

My dear Friend, Isabella Westlake had written, *How can I begin to describe to you the beauty of this place, with its brilliant, multi-coloured flora and dramatic vistas of rock and mountain? But then, of course, you are already familiar with these exquisite sights from your sojourn of last year, which now seems so long ago. No doubt the poignancy of my situation here sharpens and renews the powers of observation, as the contemplation of these things never ceases or fails to afford consolation and even delight in the very midst of the desolation in which I languish, so far from my friends and from all that is dear to me. I am resigned to the knowledge that my life is unlikely to be a long one, and probably within a very few years I shall be no more. And yet, despite the injunctions and admonitions of religion to those in my circumstances, I cannot but resent the loving kindness and care which has brought me here and consigned me to this exquisitely lovely place with none but the very best of intentions. For, if I can purchase a longer lease on life only by the absence of much of what has made it worth living... That, I genuinely believe, I prefer not to do.*

But enough of this. Tell me, my dearest Harriet, how you do these blissful days of Spring? ...'Whan longen folk to goon on pilgrimages/And palmers for to seken straunge strondes/To ferne halwes kowth in sundry londes...'

I shall address this to you in town, as it should reach you more swiftly from there even if you are in the country. Meanwhile I take the air here, and peruse and devour my beloved novelists, and swallow what I am required to swallow, and long for you, and for the others. I hear that dear little Sophie de Varnes is to marry one of our fellow countrymen, a baronet from Norfolk, of whom I know nothing. I rejoice for her, for the tenor of things here could make one uneasy.

Write, my dearest Harriet, as I know you will. I long to hear from you.

Your loving Isabella

Dear, desolate, phthisic Isabella, from whose Provençal refuge Harriet had sallied forth over fearsome mountain passes to her ecstatic rendezvous with Fabrizio the love magician in his bower of enchantment high on the great lake of Garda, the *Benacus* from which his noble name derived. Poor Isabella, sustained only by the pale blandishments of her beloved Richardson and Mr Fielding. Harriet readily acknowledged the plea in her friend's letter, and tried to imagine what it must be like to live in awareness of ones own likely imminent demise. She decided she simply could not, and gave up on that. But where *desolation* was concerned ... The brilliant, fashionable Mrs de Savigny knew all about that, as much indeed as anyone ever, and about the humiliation of being cast off by even such a man as Peter de Savigny, a monster of vice and depravity despite appearances who really was, it seemed, beyond helping himself, and who was beginning to bear an uncanny resemblance to certain *quasi*-grotesques in the popular cartoons of the day. And, oh, the contrast with Fabrizio, a lover and a man so far removed from her husband in virtually every way that signified that he might almost have been of a different species!

But she had resolved, once that had come to an end, that there was to be no dwelling in maudlin self-pity upon any aspect of that relationship. What Fabrizio di Benaco had taught her and showed her about the practice of love and about herself had been absorbed into the palimpsest persona that was Harriet de Savigny. It would live on in her, and her life would be the richer for what it might continue to contribute, as it would contribute, one way or another through her, to enrich her daughter's, Charlotte's existence in the next generation. On that Harriet was determined; Fabrizio's gift of knowledge and experience had been inestimable in its value, and Harriet knew she would honour her former lover every day for the rest of her life. Thus, in due course, Charlotte should enter into that inheritance by virtue of a legacy of awareness, a gift to her future womanhood, as it were.

None of which, however, came anywhere near to solving the most immediate and mundane but pressing of her problems, the question of money.

Harriet had been born to substantial wealth at the level of prosperous gentry, and Lord Hawkhurst had been more than generous in his provision for the wife and daughter of his feckless son, *but the demands of the kind of fashionable metropolitan life which the Hawkhursts did not frequent and within which Harriet had come to move and have her being more or less as of right could be seen to be stretching well beyond her means.* This could, she knew, become a formidable if not insurmountable obstacle to the realisation of ambitious dreams which were as yet no more than embryonic. So Harriet, of late, with more than a little trepidation which soon developed into an exhilarating addiction to risk, had taken to gambling in circles which she could not afford to frequent but which, flatteringly, had welcomed her most cordially. And little by little she had allowed herself to be drawn – by such as Mr Fox, the Duchess of Devonshire and sometimes even the Prince of Wales himself – into a spiral of commitment in debt which she knew despite herself could not but increase.

This then was the magnificent Mrs de Savigny, who had gorged herself, in relief and delight at his unworldly innocence, on the youthful male virility of her nephew, Sebastian Haverhill, somewhat more than ten years her junior, and in knowledge of virtually everything, a mere child by comparison with her. But Sebastian was decidedly well-endowed, enthusiastic and eager to be schooled in such erotic arts as she could impart, and as their embrace had become union, and she had coaxed him to a delirious, shared paroxysm – with the thought of Fabrizio in the back of her mind as invariably – a particular notion of how she might go about implementing her intention vis-à-vis the Hawkhurst inheritance had begun to take shape in her mind.

PARIS
1785

And thus it was that the Fairfax berlin was now making its
way across the bare reaches of northern France and on down
towards the more welcoming regions of the Ile de France and
Paris itself.

Between them, to Julian's private satisfaction, the young
men had begun almost immediately they had reached *terra
firma* again to pick out aspects of difference between features
of the new landscapes they now traversed and what was
familiar back at home. The elaborate bell-towers of churches
and public buildings, and the *carillon* refrains from the former
which marked the hours and their divisions – recalled by Julian
from the time of his own first ventures afield in young manhood
as something almost timeless in the way they characterised
that part of France and the Low Countries – Flanders, Artois,
Picardy – were remarked upon, as were the unhedged, rolling,
wind-swept farmlands and, most particularly by Sebastian, the
gaunt, ghastly, starved appearance of the poor folk of the
villages and small towns through which they passed.

"No-one on my Father's estate goes without shoes, by
God!" said Edward. "Mother sees to all that."

"Indeed, my boy. And there lies one of the most glaring of
the differences between us," said Julian.

"But, sir?"

"Sebastian?"

"Where are the great landlords, the estate owners? Do
they exercise no concern for their people?"

"They are at Court at Versailles, or in town, sir. And the answer to your second question is 'very little' – with the occasional honourable exception."

"Monsieur and Madame de Ménars?"

"Indeed. And others. But it is not like home, over here. The philosophy of land ownership differs, and with it the moral attitudes of the French *noblesse"*, and here Julian allowed his thoughts to dwell briefly upon the wretched condition, the misery of the labouring folk, with its potential, as he saw it, for desperate initiatives. He began, provisionally, to pen in his mind his first missive back to Lord Temple at the Foreign Office in London.

"A fact-finding mission, my dear Greenwood," that politician had said. "Take note, sir, of everything. Your observations will afford us valuable intelligence on the present condition of what I surmise must surely be a most unhappy country."

"But, gentlemen," Julian went on, "one brief cautionary word, if I may. We travel as foreign visitors in this country. You, Sebastian, have as yet only a modest knowledge of the language. You, Edward, have little if any, as far as I have ascertained... no, no, sir, if you please," Julian warded off an intervention from Ned. "In such circumstances, unless one guards against it, there can be an inclination on the part of the unschooled and unwary to mock and sneer too readily at what is only imperfectly perceived and understood. But you shall guard against this, if you please, in the interest of that true dignity which accords with your rank as gentlemen. We travel, sirs, to acquire this kind of knowledge, which makes for a cosmopolitan understanding of different ways of living, and indeed the experience and recollection of this Tour should enhance, *in perpetuo* as it were, ones sense of what life is, and can be. I should be sad if ours were to amount to nothing more than a prolonged comedy show. And, Edward, when you come to do your stint in the Guards, as I understand it is most likely you may, you will perhaps recall these words of mine when you consider how particularly rigorously common soldiers have to be disciplined when campaigning abroad."

"For these reasons, sir?"

"Indeed, for these reasons. Military campaigns, remember do have their being within a larger context of politics. Officers should act out of this kind knowledge – not that they invariably do. But one should never allow oneself to forget that military action of what-ever kind on whatever scale has its place within that larger political framework in which attitudes towards accommodation may be conditioned by recollection of outrage, or otherwise. But, more of that some other time." Julian smiled at the two boys, having that Edward might have been on the point of taking offence. And what a prickly fellow he was, that young man. But Lord Withybrook had delegated his parental responsibility to him, Julian Greenwood, and the boy should receive such instruction – and admonition where necessary – as he, Julian, *in loco parentis,* should see fit to mete out.

"So, Farrell, it is to be the Guards, then?"

"Just so, man. Just so."

"Then may you prosper and thrive, sir, and become... A general, and things."

"Do you mock me, sir?"

"No, my dear old Ned, I do not. Not for the world. Not this time."

"Very well, sir."

Ned, placated, allowed his scowl of distrust and suspicion to become a smile of some warmth in response to the obvious affection of Sebastian's denial. Julian, observing from his vantage point, allowed himself some wry private amusement at the disparity between the two young men and the closeness of their friendship despite that.

The carriage trundled on its way through a small town characterised by many a fine bourgeois dwelling, for the most part well maintained and often freshly painted, which lined the highway. Around the main square stood public buildings which bespoke a degree of pride and self-regard as well as prosperity. Beyond the town, forest became visible, as the road led, arrow-like, towards it.

"We appear, sir, to have put the high plateau behind us."

"True, Sebastian. This is the beginning of the Ile de France, gentlemen, the very core of the old kingdom of France itself. Much of the forest is royal, reserved for hunting, and we shall soon be seeing more in the way of châteaux and fine houses, some of them very fine indeed."

"Sir?"

"Yes, Edward?"

"Do they hunt fox, as we do?"

"No, no, my boy. Stag, mainly."

The expression on Edward's face brought a smile to Julian's.

"And would you be about to inquire whether there might any chance...?"

"Precisely that, sir. Precisely that."

"When we reach the Loire, sir. At my cousin's."

"I've hunted there, sir. With Philippe and Aurélien."

"I do not doubt it, Sebastian," Julian laughed with delight at his kinsman's mention of the young French cousins.

"From what I hear, those two are hardly ever out of the saddle, and quite right , too. Young men should hunt, by God! But I was about to say, gentlemen, that tonight we shall put up virtually within striking distance of Paris itself. Then tomorrow we shall enjoy domesticity again, the hospitality of Edward's French cousins. Some respite from the road will not come amiss, I think."

"No, indeed, sir," said both young men.

"And Maître Courtois, sir?"

"Early next week, Edward. After a spot of recuperation, if I may so word it – and as a reward for your patience in other matters."

"May one inquire, what other matters?"

"Looking at paintings," said Sebastian.

"And sculpture, and architecture. Oh, and Edward..."

"Sir?"

"You may be sure that where the latter are concerned, there will be military considerations, of the sorts of things an officer should know about. Siege techniques, for instance."

"I shall be cavalry, sir."

"No doubt. But consider, when you command the higher echelons, if you ever do, you will need to understand the coordination of cavalry, infantry, engineers, artillery..."

"I had not thought of that, sir."

"Then do, sir. Think of it and prepare for it. The sooner the better."

*

The carriage made its way through the outer *quartiers* and on into the teeming streets of the French capital. There was much about the appearance of these thoroughfares that was familiar to the young men from London – the noisy markets, the open sewers running with pungent filth, the masses of folk of the poorer kind together with the appalling stench – here, if anything more noisome – that they bore with them. And the whole converged upon the mighty Seine, river of legend and verse, where the monumental buildings of the historic centre clustered on and round the two islands – Notre-Dame de Paris, the Conciergerie prison, the Louvre palace. And above all there was the noise – of humanity multiplied by many a thousand from the single individual – going about its business, its daily occasions.

After their time spent covering the open road and unfamiliar countryside, the homely roar of the metropolis was like a welcome to the two young men, while Mr Greenwood, more seasoned in his experience of such ventures abroad, looked forward to hot water, clean linen, a finer, more comfortable style of dress, and the enjoyment of dinner and a sojourn among hosts of a class and style close to his own. He recalled his own brief years of service as a military officer, the unpredictable character of a billet in the field, the often heterogeneous ambiance of a mess on campaign, and the relief and pleasure of the homecoming, of finding oneself once again among friends and family. And yet the lure of the unknown never did lose its power, and the anticipation of the drive across France, down to the Loire and his own cousins, on through the mountains and into Provence and then Italy was as fresh as ever. Meanwhile, decent wine and conversation would come as most welcome, assuming Edward's French relatives were equal to the lad's social pretensions. Julian look forward to this first evening of their arrival in Paris.

And so it proved to be. At the Hôtel de Châtigny, town residence of Lady Withybrook's French cousins, they were welcomed by Monsieur le Comte and his lady and a substantial family of cousins and associates and taken in with much excited chatter. Julian's travelling servants were appropriately and properly accommodated, and the three gentlemen received into the family circle.

Later that evening, after a brief sortie into the immediate environs with Edward's cousin, Gautier -"Dark cloaks, gentlemen, and we go armed, if you please!"- Sebastian penned his impressions of their arrival in France and its capital city.

We were struck, Ned and I, from the moment we landed on French soil, by *what can only be described as the utter difference in appearance of landscape, buildings and people. One could have scarcely have believed it possible that, at a distance of no more than twenty-odd miles of water, the character of this land and its people could be simply so alien. For, the landscape differs because it is husbanded according to different principles; the architecture likewise – as far as one can ascertain – has its own very particular and distinctive variations on common themes. We have not, for instance, so far espied anything remotely resembling a Palladian villa among the finer houses. Additionally, the common people look distinctly less well off, less well-nourished and less contented than do our own at home; where we in England share a sense of identity which transcends distinctions of rank; where Ned, the heir to great wealth and a fine title of nobility, can try conclusions with a mercenary mauler from the stews of South London to the approbation and thorough approval of all and sundry, from the fine gentlemen at White's to the urchins wagering coppers at the ringside, one perceives no similar affinities among the French. One does swiftly become aware of this difference, of the way they so disconcertingly stand away from each other in their respective stations, and such awareness does not make for comfort. I must discuss this with my knowledgeable Uncle Greenwood sometime before long.*

If one is to be entirely frank and open, as one should be within the confidential bounds of a diary, it was not, it must be said, without some trepidation, certainly on my part, that we arrived at the Hôtel de Châtigny to make the acquaintance of Nedward's cousins – that is to say, relatives of some degree of distance, but 'cousins' to the French nevertheless – a gracious usage, it seems to me - Monsieur and Madame de Châtigny and family, of whom, in detail, more later. Fine people, though, let it be said at once. Polished in manner and unassumingly agreeable. I could see that my Uncle Greenwood was hugely reassured by the manner of our reception, and most especially by the personal style and 'ton' of the Count and his lady. As, equally, they took to him, most probably in the first instance by virtue of his accomplished command of their language. Of course, it has long been the custom amongst our gentry and aristocracy to speak French with some degree of mastery, but degrees can vary, and here there was no question of anything less than total. One could observe how they warmed to him and – if I may add this – to my rather less capable efforts also. The eldest son, Gautier, who led our brief sally into the environs after dinner, does speak some English too, so we have already established an amiable rapport. There are two younger boys, Thibault and Guillaume, aged fourteen and twelve respectively, a daughter, Clothilde, of seventeen or so, and two little girls, Diane and Elisabeth, who giggled and whispered until they were removed by a nurse-like person.

Given the pèrennial fascination of genealogy, I must establish the exact nature of the connection between them and Ned, who did actually endeavour to make some sort of an effort at French at table – largely, I suspect, in the interest of his seventeen-year old 'cousine', who coaxed him along with the most enchanting subtlety, and thanks to whom he probably even surprised himself with what he knew. But I shall say nothing of this to him; he is so damnably sensitive of possible mockery. I know, also, that my Uncle Greenwood has seen and appreciated this aspect of him; at all events he does seem to make a point of showing approval of and interest in Ned, which old Withybrook never did, not to my knowledge anyway, and I have stayed frequently in Warwickshire. How a man may be expected to grow into a stature both moral and social, which may be commensurate with a notion of rank held with distinction when he is in constant receipt of criticism and abuse it is hard to imagine. I know my Uncle Greenwood is of similar opinion – he too knows his Greeks and his Florentine Humanists, one senses this in what is evident of his idea of a 'mentor'. And indeed, to my way of thinking, the discovery that one who was fondly assumed - and I use the word 'fondly' with deliberate, self-deprecating intent here – in so far as one assumed anything much, to be a homespun north-country squire with the corollary, albeit implicit, of homespun manners and the speech to go with them à la Western in Mr Fielding's novel, is actually a gentleman of urbane manners and excellent learning and knowledge of the world has been, for me, one of the most profoundly enlightening insights of our venture so far. One is altogether too inclined, I think, to make assumptions based on nothing more than notions of type. One should guard against this, in moral judgment, and go only by direct experience. Perhaps this is what is meant by 'knowing the world'? I allow that I had not considered the matter in this light before this moment.

We are to remain with the Châtignys for our first week here in Paris, by the end of which time the lodgings provisionally bespoken for us by Mr Greenwood through the agency of a French connection of his own will have been inspected and approved – or not, as the case may be. Meanwhile, I have a mind to speak to Ned's cousin, Gautier, about the possibility of some riding; the best part of a week spent crammed inside a carriage leaves one decidedly in need of some such outdoor activity. Perhaps, also, while it occurs to me, we might invite cousin Gautier to accompany us to the Courtois rendezvous, for it is said, I know, that the subtlety of the French in the art of swordplay is greatly to be admired. No doubt they see us as raw Anglo-Saxons who ply the technique of the battle-axe, but we shall make a point of disabusing them there. Mr Greenwood a Viking beserker? I think not. Most decidedly not.

Over the next few days we are to make a point of acquainting ourselves with the most noteworthy features of this historic place, to acquire a rudimentary sense of the topography, and the situation of key landmarks. And I have to say that, although this is not my first visit to France - I have sojourned on one previous occasion with the Fairfax cousins at Ménars – everything this time does strike me as novel and of especial and particular interest. I surmise this has to do with the character of the larger enterprise upon which we are engaged; we are not simply on a visit to Paris this time, but at the first stage of a Grand Tour which will incorporate many other places of at least equal interest and aesthetic and historical appeal. And indeed, the prospect of a continuing feast of such riches is, when one considers it, almost over-whelming; it is an experience, this, which needs to be approached in leisurely, thoughtful style, otherwise the kaleidoscope of impressions which will surely take shape – if one may appropriate an image with the help of the Greek – will quite simply degenerate into something too zany to be of lasting value. I shall make a point, therefore, of savouring the French experience, then the Italian, then the German. In this respect Ned is a great support, for in his matter of fact way he takes everything in his stride and goes by his instinct for things, as for instance earlier this evening, when he was prompted to attempt some converse in French, which otherwise he would never have done, with his pretty cousin, Clothilde, who was so enchantingly gracious to him and tactful over his efforts, to boot. Truly, the manners of such as the Châtignys must be without compare anywhere in the civilised world. And I have to say that the wonder of all this, the experience which the Tour is already providing should, cherished in the memory, enrich ones future existence immeasurably by what it cannot but afford in the way of recollection of such delight. I wonder, as an afterthought, just where exactly Châtigny is, and how the poor folk do there.

FRANCE
1785

The same thought had briefly occurred to Julian Greenwood as, alone now after a cordial evening with the Count and his lady, he pottered happily about his chamber before preparing for bed. Unlike his nephew, however, Julian did know where Châtigny was to be found – just about on the Normandy side of the great divide, frontier almost, between that region and the ancient, proudly independent dukedom of Brittany, within easy reach of the mighty medieval stronghold of Fougères, and less than a morning's ride from Vitré, where a similarly intimidating fortress, equally grim and purposeful, guarded a further stretch of that divide. But there were other, more cheering associations too, for Vitré, as he now recalled, adjoined a tiny spot named Argentré du Plessis, notable only for the Château des Rochers, where Madame de Sévigné some hundred or so years previously had penned her exquisite letters to her beloved daughter in Provence.

Tomorrow should be a day of relaxation, with perhaps a modest tour on foot of the *cité* with its most noteworthy monuments. Julian, a bachelor and a solitary who was perfectly contented with his lot, was not so unaccustomed to the younger members of his own family as not to have noted the eagerness with which Sebastian and Edward had acquiesced in Gautier de Châtigny's proposal that they stretch their legs a little after dinner, and the alacrity with which they complied with his advice that they arm themselves against possible affray. And it occurred to Julian now that it might well be quite possible that

that young man would not have been averse to a spot of affray, had it offered itself. But if that was the case, he could join them at the *salle d'armes,* or take them on at the *jeu de paume*, or at least at other forms of lawful engagement. Julian understood that it would be vital to keep them occupied and busy, and wryly looked forward to a strenuous two years. The experience of the Tour should be most carefully orchestrated, and conducted at a pace congenial to all of them; any attempt to cram in everything could result only in irritation and disenchantment. Julian, sufficiently familiar with what Paris had to offer, resolved to speak to Gilbert de Châtigny, his host, about a possible visit to the Court at Versailles, to encourage the young men to exercise with tennis, swordplay and riding in the Bois de Boulogne, or indeed, if feasible, in the forests around the periphery of the great capital – Saint Cloud, Marly, Vincennes.

He recalled his own delight of some twenty years previously, his own Tour of France and Italy and the taste for travel he had acquired from it. And as he did so, the current enterprise began to take shape in his mind, in the contemplation of, first, the sojourn at Paris – several weeks most likely, but no longer than they were inclined, to do the things one did there. To visit the Court of France at Versailles and catch at least a glimpse of the King – he awaited official support from Lord Temple at the Foreign Office via the Paris Embassy there; to attend the *salle d'armes* of Maître Courtois on a regular basis, in order to effect significant improvement in the boys' knowledge and practice of the art of fence; to ride in the Bois and to make new acquaintance in society, through the Châtignys and through his own connections; to view such art and architecture as they may see fit, and to make progress in the French language. All in all an undertaking ambitious enough, Julian appreciated. Months would not be enough to encompass all of it, and he was keen to see his own Fairfax cousin, Sophie de Ménars and his old friend, her husband Charles and their family in the Loire Valley. But Ménars should be the next stage, a country interlude after the more intensive life of the metropolis. Then, the mountains. A long and irksome journey, although thinking back to Madame de Sévigné he recalled that this indomitable lady and tenderly loving mother had travelled from Brittany to Grignan in northern Provence and back not once but several times. Perhaps they might entertain the notion of picking up on her route? That was something to be borne in mind. So, the mountains, Provence and the ancient Roman sites there, and then, eventually, Italy. By the sea route after all, perhaps, rather than through yet more mountains? That would bring them within striking distance of the old cities of those northern regions – Lucca, Pistoia, Pisa, Florence... The further stages of the venture could be worked out in due course. There was also the very real possibility that Harriet would put in an appearance sooner or later. Of that he was sure. For whatever her reasons might be for such excursions as he knew her to make, she was frequently known to be abroad and about France and Italy. A discontented nomad, he assumed, in the aftermath of her disastrous marriage to that hopeless oaf who had given her nothing but a daughter and a splendid name.

And having marshalled his thoughts on all these matters, Julian turned with relief to the essays of Michel de Montaigne, a provincial *seigneur* very much of his own ilk, who spoke to him across two hundred years of preoccupations and deliberations not at all unfamiliar.

*

From Hawkhurst House with its view from the north side of Piccadilly across to the Park, Harriet de Savigny penned a letter to her ailing friend, Isabella Westlake.

My dearest Isabella, she wrote, *I have received your last, as I was already here in my favourite part of town when it arrived. I have to say that I grieve at the sadness I sense in your lines, and will do all that is in my power to bring you out of that. And a propos, my Cousin Greenwood, he of Bowland, Lancashire, has engaged - largely at my behest, I have to say - to accompany my young nephew, Sebastian, whom you may recall as a somewhat grubby if engaging youth, and a school friend, Edward Farrell, son of that awful old satyr Withybrook, whom you may also recall, albeit for quite different reasons, on a Tour of France and Italy and quite possibly a number of the German principalities too. I know for instance that my Cousin Greenwood, a somewhat enigmatic and rather formidable figure, of impeccable social credentials but nonetheless not entirely unequivocal standing in Town circles, has links of strong affection which bind him to, of all places, Berlin, a city - with its emblem of the Bear, would you believe it? - which to my way of thinking lies so far to the eastward as to be virtually in Russia! My brother Simon, who languishes at home in Hertfordshire, was most reluctant to allow the project to go forward; he had long cherished hopes that my nephew, now a most elegant young gentleman, would take the King's commission when the time came and follow the colours as he himself had done. As if Sebastian were cut out for that kind of life, despite his, or indeed our military antecedents! Be that all as it may, however, the travelling party is now at Paris enjoying the initial stages of their sojourn there under the auspices of the Count and Countess de Châtigny, excellent people who I know a little through the d'Aubignacs. (Do you recall our wonderful gallop that time at Marly, with Genevieve d'Aubignac? And neither she nor I realised you had never attempted anything of that kind before! Which probably comes of not having brothers! But, how wonderfully courageous you were that day, my darling Isabella, and how positively daunting the whole thing must have seemed!)*

Do please bear with me in your accustomed sweet way, as I meander through family anecdote and personal reminiscence. You may feel yourself very much alone in that lovely place high above the gorgeous Mediterranean; I am no less alone here in the teeming heart of old London Town. I shall say nothing of my husband, Peter. There is simply nothing I care to say of him. I am finding the strength to make my own way without him – with the assistance of the fine name which was his only endowment, apart from darling Charlotte, of course. And I do most passionately hope that you too will find the strength to contend with the malady which assails you. Do you recall how, as little girls, we would cuddle in the darkness? What bliss! What solace to be gained from such closeness! For tears shared are never quite so bitter as tears shed alone. And oh, that appalling academy! A correspondence such as this, conducted over great distances, can never quite compensate for the absence of that kind of intimate affection, but perhaps it may go some way towards alleviating the pain of solitude and melancholy. I shall make my way down to you once the turn of the year is past. I call first - after Paris, that is upon the Fairfax cousins at Ménars, where our travellers will shortly celebrate Christmas. And after that, I shall take 'the most direct route' (remember?) to you, my darling. Your ever affectionate...

Harriet signed and sanded her letter, after which she remained seated, lost in her thoughts, gazing out across the Park. If Isabella were to die, she mused, she would all too rapidly become a mere recollection of love irretrievable. Set against that, Harriet realised, her other problems were as nothing. And she did have her fine name to conjure with, in the fickle world of society. Thus, even in the desolation of her abandoned situation and of her virtually certain knowledge that her beloved friend would be taken from her before her time, Harriet de Savigny began to sense something of her own strength, and to exult in it with a wild and fierce delight.

She would arrange a rendezvous with the Greenwood party, most likely at Venice during Carnival in just over a year's time. And there she would contrive the means of having Sebastian to herself for just long enough... Assuming Peter were still alive by that time, it would be easy enough to fabricate a tale of plausible encounter subsequently to be dismissed by her as having been a regrettable error... And with the guise of anonymity *in maschera,* and the riot and dissipation of the moment, Sebastian would be a ready quarry, given his certain recollection of the delight of their previous encounters. Meanwhile, as always, there was the vexed question of money.

*

In Paris, Edward Farrell was in process of penning a letter to his mother in Warwickshire, but as composition did not come easily to him, he preferred to approach the matter gradually and punctuate his efforts with recollections of what had been after all a most memorable day. For that morning the Greenwood party, accompanied by Gautier de Châtigny, had made the acquaintance of Maître Courtois, the legendary fencing master of the Rue des Francs Bourgeois, in whose *salle d'armes* the actuality of practice had more than matched up to expectations. For one could not but be impressed, as Sebastian had remarked at the time, by the atmosphere of decorum and dedication in which the fencing exercises were conducted - by Maître Courtois himself and two younger, gifted assistants, former Army sergeants both, whose natural sense of what was involved in the skilled practice of swordplay had been espied by the Master and put to use accordingly.

There had been perhaps a dozen or so gentlemen at practice that morning - gentlemen of a range of ages and degrees of skill, carefully paired off to complement one another in matters of technique, to practise particular sequences of movement and the subtler measures of rhythm, timing and deceit which may be exercised through foot-work to foil anticipation and effect an opening for attack. It soon became clear that Gautier de Châtigny was already well versed in Courtois techniques when Sebastian found himself hit three times in as many passes before he had even begun to realise how this had been effected. At the fourth pass however, Sebastian found himself actually luring his adversary into the same style of attack, finding the parry and scoring his own on the *riposte.* At the fifth exchange Gautier hit him again.

"Gentlemen, if you please!"

When Maître Courtois addressed the fencers he had their instant attention. Only the previous week, Gautier informed and Sebastian and Edward, the scion of a great family had been summarily dismissed from the *salle* for less than immediate compliance.

"Unmannerly petulance, sir! Quite out of place here, or indeed anywhere. You may leave, sir, and return when you know how to behave like a gentleman."

Courtois had made an enemy for the public humiliation, but the boy's father had himself written a note of apology.

Sebastian and Gautier saluted, unmasked, shook hands left-handed as right-handed swordsmen do.

"Good, gentlemen. Good, Monsieur Haverhill. You were quick to find a defence against M. de Châtigny after your first exchanges, but how was it, can you explain to me, that he hit you a fourth time just now?"

The Fencing Master's English was smooth, practised, and idiomatic in the style of his class, only slightly accented.

"I am still trying to account for it, Monsieur," said Sebastian.

"And you, Monsieur Greenwood, did you observe, sir?"

"I did, Maître, yes."

"Well, then?"

Slight in build as he was, insignificant in terms of bulk, there was nevertheless an assumption of absolute mastery and command in Courtois' manner and utterance. In the first instance it was, Sebastian understood, most likely a military thing, but at a deeper level it derived from an understanding and mastery of what began as a science, a matter of technicality and technique, and came in due course to be an art, a celebration of fine intelligence and rapid thinking *à l'improviste* based on what laborious exercise had transformed into an almost instinctive command of movement, timing, speed and coordination. Sebastian marvelled.

"A most promising young man, my dear Greenwood. What a pity your visit must be so brief."

"True, Maître. But perhaps we may attend on a regular basis for as long as we are in Paris?"

"You are most welcome, sir. But now, your other young man, who has waited so patiently. Mr Farrell, if you please..."

My dear Mamma, Edward wrote, *We have reached Paris, where we stay for the moment with M. and Mme de Châtigny, who have made us most welcome. The Hôtel de Châtigny is an elegant residence of truly aristocratic character, the family genteel and refined and – can you imagine? – I have been speaking French to my cousins, Gautier and Clothilde, who send you their respectful salutations. If you are able to write me a reply to this (please address to Ménars, as we arrive there within the month) could you please find out from William how Jenny has done with her pups and let me know? He is not to dispose of any, unless infirm, until I learn of the contents of the litter, and then decide. Also, would you be so good as to send a man, Longwood, say, to Jones the blacksmith to attend to my hunters, Satan and Lysander, and Reuben not to feed them too hearty, unless after exercise.*

We have been exercising today with Courtois, the great fencing master of Paris; were we to sojourn here longer, Sebastian and I should become passably adept; I say 'passably' because the French ply the blade with surpassing skill, including cousin Gautier. Mr Greenwood fought a bout with the Maître, and everybody in the salle came to watch, and applauded, and truly, this was something quite out of the ordinary. Mr Greenwood, Sebastian's kinsman, is a fine gentleman, and speaks languages and seems to know the world to a fair degree. He is a gentleman of accomplishment, and as such a worthy mentor. He too sends you his greeting. I am Madam, your most affectionate son, Edward Farrell.

His letter completed, Edward sat back from the table he had been so laboriously crouched over and thought about his cousin, Clothilde de Châtigny. An accomplished lady in the making, of that there was no question, but there was more to his pretty cousin than that. Up to now, Edward's experience of the female sex had consisted very largely of casual encounters with women not of his own class in circumstances decidedly rackety. Bought encounters, he had to allow, and of the sensations of tender emotion Edward as yet knew nothing. But he did know that there could be no equivocal approaches where Clothilde was concerned. Ladies of her kind were sacrosanct, guarded by a ring of brothers and kinsmen who would be only too happy, given the prevalence of the duelling custom in France, to call a man out and kill him. Edward had watched his cousin, Gautier, at fence with Sebastian with the dispassionate eye of the technician, a style of observation developed through his pugilistic pursuits, and he knew without any doubt at all that in serious swordplay he was simply no match for the Frenchman. At fisticuffs it might well be a different matter, he told himself with some satisfaction and recovery of self-regard, even as it registered with him that any French gentleman of quality would most likely look with supercilious disdain upon such a plebeian method of settling matters between protagonists. But besides, any attempt to seduce Clothilde was just not to be contemplated; the frank, open warmth of her welcome, her apparently genuine interest in him, her patience with his stumbling efforts to converse in her language put her into a category of person Edward had only rarely met with but invariably did respond to, people who seemed at least to take a genuine interest in him for himself. There had been Reuben, the stable-boy at Withybrook now charged with the care of Edward's precious hunters, who had first taught him the use of his fists. Cook, who had fed him, a lonely, hungry little boy, with quantities of left-over rabbit pie, and now this exquisitely refined young French lady. So, he reasoned, he must aim to please her in legitimate ways, by acting decently towards her, making an effort at the French language, showing an interest in her in the way she showed an interest in him. Briefly he regretted not having worked at this French in the way Sebastian always had; for all the apparent priggishness of him, Haverhill had a point there, Edward now saw, although to do himself justice, one had hardly anticipated the delights of social intercourse with such as Mademoiselle de Châtigny during the years squandered at Westminster.

And then there was Mr Greenwood. Edward Farrell had grown to manhood deeply imbued with the notion, which he had from his father, that only men of superior rank and title counted for anything in the world. But here was this gentleman, this obscure Lancashire squire, totally at home in the polished *milieux* of fashionable London and aristocratic Paris, a swordsman of superlative quality judged even by the very best, a connoisseur of languages, a scholar... and what else Edward just did not know, but instinct told him he had not plumbed the depths of Julian Greenwood yet, nothing like.

And that evening, Edward Farrell began for the first time to question the conventional notion of an equation between rank and human quality; it was as if his tender appreciation of the sweet cousin now no doubt fast asleep elsewhere in the house had somehow opened up a whole new area of moral perception. And he thought again of the Mangler, Venus, with his "I shall remember you, young gentleman," and of Cook and the rabbit pie, of Reuben who first taught him the use of his fists, of Clothilde's tactful correction of a phrase over which he had halted, and found himself aware of a quite special sense of elation, and one such as he had only rarely known ever before.

*

... And you will remember, my Lord, how in the aftermath of the noble rebellion of the Fronde of last century King Louis XIV contrived quite deliberately to create, in the new royal palace of Versailles, such a magnificent setting for his presence as to draw the nobles to him, thus detaching them from their country estates in order that they might live under his ever distrustful surveillance as they attended to their trivial duties about the royal residence, the very seat of power. In this way the King was able to clip their wings politically but - it now emerges - at enormous cost in terms of the wealth and well-being of the country at large. Not least in these terms was the fatal - in my view - neglect of the proper practice of husbandry with, now, the effects of this all too apparent in the miserable condition of the labouring people, whose sullen, starved aspect was sufficient to draw comment quite unprompted from Mr Farrell as well as from my own nephew.

It is now more than a decade since hostilities between our two countries came to an end. In the circles in which we move here in Paris we have been made most generously welcome by well-nourished gentlefolk of ostentatious opulence and polished manners. But they contrive, these fine folk, somehow to intimate that they feel themselves closer in their affinities to us, their social equals from Outre Manche, than they do to the vast majority of their own population, whom they regard with a contempt which does jar most dreadfully. I sense, in addition, an anxiety in Gilbert de Châtigny – although we have not touched specifically upon such matters – for his family, its future and posterity, and over what may transpire to affect them one way or another in their adult lives at a time beyond his own demise when he

*will no longer be at hand to afford them his loving
protection.*

*I trust, my Lord, that deliberations of this nature were
what you had in mind when you invited me to contribute
observations and opinions on the present state of
France as we made our way through the country. I
shall therefore continue to furnish you with such on a
regular if occasional basis as we go about our private
purposes.*

Julian paused to rest his eyes from the candlelight and
cut a new quill; he would make his letter over personally
to a diplomatic acquaintance at the Embassy in Faubourg
St Honoré, trusting it to be conveyed via the usual diplomatic
channels to Lord Temple at the Foreign Office in London.
Now he brought matters to a swift, succinct conclusion.
Time for a quick look at Madame de Sévigné, and leisurely
search through the *Letters* for references to the route she
would have taken from Les Rochers in Ille et Vilaine to
Grignan in Drôme Provençale. The idea of making use of
it themselves did rather have its appeal. From somewhere
beyond the Loire and Ménars, obviously. Somewhere south
of the river.

*

Within the week the travelling party had taken leave, with many
repeated promises to return, of the Châtigny family and moved
into lodgings of their own in the Faubourg St Germain. A suite
of rooms , with the services of a jolly, rubicund landlady,
Madame Bernard, and her little staff became their comfortable,
unpretentious base for continued visits to Maître Courtois, tennis
at the Jeu de Paume, riding in the Bois with such members of
the Châtigny family as cared to make themselves available,
which meant effectively all but Madame and the little girls.

Julian Greenwood, drawing upon his military experience of
twenty years previously, found himself eyeing the health of

Sebastian and Edward as he might once have done that of his men on campaign. The outdoor exercise and the regular exertions of *salle d'armes* and tennis court had dispelled the costive pallor brought on by even those few initial confinements to the coach over the journey from London to Paris. Young men, like young bullocks, needed to be fostered with unremitting care if they were not to do themselves harm, one way or another. And there was much to be said in favour of a good gallop over suitable terrain.

By now the bright sunshine of autumn over Paris was beginning to give way to what was effectively a more chill reminder of winter to come. Julian recalled the countryside of Touraine, frost in the trees, snow on the ground, the conviviality of the Château de Ménars, the warmth and *bonhomie* of the Seigneur, Charles de Ménars, a kinsman by his marriage to Julian's cousin, Sophia Fairfax, now Sophie de Ménars, a friend of long standing, and of the labouring folk as they celebrated the successful hunting of boar and stag with huge communal feasting. And much as he loved the life of the town, whether London or Paris or indeed elsewhere, the blood and sensibilities of the country squire soon led him to yearn longingly back to that, and all that went with it.

Meanwhile, though, there was one major event to be anticipated before they could be about their next move onwards - the visit to the Court at Versailles.

Their *entrée* to what was to prove a spectacle every bit as glittering as anticipation might wish to make it, to the actual presence of the King and his family, had been engineered through the good offices of Gilbert de Châtigny in reinforcing intimations from London via the Embassy that such favour would be greatly appreciated and not forgotten. As he dressed and groomed himself for the occasion Julian spared one wry thought in passing for the apparent *insouciance* of the young men who had spent their morning at the Tennis Court without a qualm, it would seem, over what the day was to bring. But there, for once, Julian had not quite hit the mark.

"Well, Haverhill, thanks to my Uncle Châtigny you are to see the King of France."

It was undoubtedly quite a thing, Sebastian acknowledged as he struggled to adjust his stock, but Farrell was not going to get away with that, as if it mattered. He knew, however, that in some way it did, even if only in the interest of his Uncle Greenwood.

"Partly, Farrell. Only partly."

"Nonsense, man. What can you mean?"

"Are you not aware then, my dear old fellow, that it was intimated through the Ambassador himself – yes, none other than – that London – yes, Farrell, London- in the person of His Britannic Majesty's Secretary of State for Foreign Affairs, would not look unkindly upon such a favour to my Uncle and his travelling companions from France Himself - *le roi lui-même, pour ainsi dire?*"

"Cut the frog, Sebastian. Are you serious?"

"Certainly I am, Nedward. It was discussed between my Uncle and M. de Châtigny, who was happy to make the particular arrangements with whatever titled flunkey it may be who fulfils that function. You were there, but otherwise engaged."

"A nobleman is not a flunkey, man."

"Is that so? Is it really? *'Go tell Court huntsman that the King will ride,'* Farrell"

"What?"

"Never mind. But, do you not recall that my Uncle explained how Louis XIV deprived his nobles of the power to rebel against him by separating them from their estates and insisting they live at Versailles to perform trivial duties for which they received amazing titles to gratify their ridiculous vanities? How would you care to be Grand Seneschal of the Piss-Pot, Farrell, and hold the appropriate receptacle for the Royal Widdle? Or perhaps you would prefer the post of Taster?"

"What, piss-taster? No, thank you, Sebastian."

"Not even royal piss?"

"Not even that."

"Just as well. It's not in my gift, you know. And anyway, that's not what the Taster does."

"So, then. Just what exactly does he do?"

"He is the Officer – note, my old Nedward, Officer with a capital 'O' – who tastes the food to be served to His Majesty before he falls to, which he does, as long as the 'Officer' has not already dropped dead, which he would do if the food had been poisoned, don't you think?"

"And it all still goes on?"

"For all I know, it may well. But you keep your eyes open, this afternoon. It should be... edifying, one way or another. Tell you what, you look at me and I'll look at you. Reciprocal inspections at close quarters, that kind of thing."

"Certainly. But, Sebastian?"

"Yes?"

"You were serious, were you not, about your uncle and the Foreign Secretary, and diplomatic channels, and what have you?"

"I was."

"Extraordinary."

"Not at all. If you knew my Uncle Greenwood as we in the family know him – or think we do and probably do not, if you see what I mean – it would not appear extraordinary at all. He has always been something of a mysterious mover..." Sebastian chuckled, "My Father does not trust him an inch. 'Just a bit too inclined to consort – note that 'consort'! – with men who never quite mean what they say, or who mean something other than what they appear to mean; they all talk in code, the scoundrels!' He was referring to diplomats, politicians, people like that. But Greenwoods have always been like that. There was one in the service of old Walsingham, you know. Walsingham Senior, no less."

"Who?"

"Francis Walsingham, and later his son, Thomas. They ran Queen Elizabeth's espionage service, mainly against Spain and the continental powers of the Catholic Church. It was once said that Philip II of Spain could not even use a piss-pot, since we're on the subject, in his own palace without Walsingham knowing about it. And it is supposed to have been a Greenwood who said it."

"So, what relation exactly is your Uncle to you?"

"His mother was a Fairfax, as is mine, and Sophie de Ménars. My maternal grandmother is a Fairfax. So there is blood connection, as there is between Aurélien and Philippe de Ménars and myself but not their father, if you see what I mean."

"So. And how did this come about then? Our tour, I mean, with your Uncle as mentor?"

"In a word, Farrell, Aunt Harriet."

"Mrs de Savigny? And that was two words, man."

"Oh, good old Nedward!"

"Don't you patronise me, man!"

"My dear old man, I wouldn't dream of it. You beat me at tennis this morning, remember?"

"Sebastian, do you know, it occurs to me that you are at serious risk of turning into one of those men your father distrusts? And good for him, I say. Soldiering's the thing, when all's said and done. That's my view."

"And just as well, if I may say so; it's also the Haverhill view, usually, that is. But do bear in mind, Ned, won't you, that men of power are without scruple in the way they will exploit the honesty of soldiers? Anyway, when is it to be?"

"In two years' time. After all this."

"And I shall look forward to the day when I may greet you as an officer, truly I shall."

"Thank you, Sebastian. And meanwhile, Mr Haverhill, shall we go and view this king of theirs?"

"This king of theirs, shall we go and view him? How very Shakespearean! 'Him' with a capital H, don't you think? And thus, circumspectly and with discretion..."

That evening Sebastian penned his diary on the visit to the Palace of Versailles.

One has to allow that, although it is most definitely not Windsor, the royal residence of the Kings of France at Versailles is not without a certain grandeur, even if this, unlike Windsor which has simply become what it is over centuries, is something rather obviously striven for. In the first instance, there are the grounds – originally conceived, it is said, on such a scale that the previous palace was just not adequate in that setting; these are meticulously landscaped into the kind of gardens with severely trimmed, close knit hedges in elaborate, sometimes over-elaborate patterns reminiscent of the Italian quattrocentro, gardens one associates with such names as Medici, Sforza, Este and other powerful families of that time. Then there are the avenues with their vistas of distant fountains and statues, framed by strategic copses of trees arranged, it seemed to me, to embody the compositional features of certain styles of painting. And there, I think, I hit upon the essence of it, further confirmed by the rituals of the Household as these are played out against the grandeur albeit a decidedly self-conscious grandeur – of the palace itself. For Versailles is a theatre, a grandiose stage set designed to manifest in visible terms the kingly power of the throne and of the individual who sits on it. And no doubt, where the originator of all this was concerned – and one is aware of what attention to the details of this, his enterprise, Louis XIV persisted in – the design worked superbly well. And thus it is that everything that we know, from whatever source, of that monarch corroborates this intention.

One is received into the Palace with positively baroque courtesy by supercilious officials, nobles of the realm directed by the hierarchy which prevails in that place to perform functions more appropriate to footmen or flunkeys - as I did have occasion to point out to Ned earlier, although I do not think he took my point and was certainly not familiar with Dr Donne's poem, The Sunne Rising.

This being so, however, les choses étant ce qu'elles sont, the French nobles are particularly sensitive to points of convoluted punctilio, and most especially where any matter pertaining to their personal rank or dignity is in question - could it perhaps have penetrated at some deeper level that successive kings have made apes of them? Within minutes of entering the royal residence Ned could scarcely contain his discomfiture and displeasure, and it took a sharp word and an exchange eye to eye between Mr Greenwood and the lackey Count who was escorting us to blunt the edge of this unhappiness – fortunately before the creature had received what would have been at least a well kicked ankle, if not a ham-like Farrell fist in the solar plexus, for then what inconveniences might so easily have transpired!

This royal residence, one feels, despite the opulence, the elegance, the fine clothes and polished manners can hardly be a happy place, with all the intrigue, the manoeuvring for advantage, the double-dealing that must surely go on around the figures of their Majesties, who in the event acknowledged us in passing with the briefest recognition. And how ordinary when viewed close up are even the great of this earth! If this particular monarch of France may be so termed, for indeed he does look as though he would rather be anything but. A podgy figure, soft of feature, over-given, one would surmise, to pleasure and self-indulgence; not one, certainly, to be taken seriously in salle d'armes or on horseback. One could hardly imagine this King putting a hunter at a hedge or a five-barred gate. What snares must superlative privilege cast in ones path! But enough. Such thoughts as these are perhaps better not recorded at any length. Although a diary is, or should be a journal of discovery. No doubt others sharper in observation and more learned than I have already noted those features of Versailles upon which I have chosen to dwell here, but the important thing, it seems to me, is that I have noted them for myself, unaided. Truly, this Tour is proving rich in edification where matters of this world are concerned. So now. One last farewell dinner and soirée at the Hôtel de Châtigny, then au revoir, Paris! Certainly, though, we shall not forget this generous, kindly family of fine aristocrats – decidedly not the Versailles type, one shudders to imagine Mademoiselle Clothilde, for instance, among the ladies of the Court – and shall look forward to returning something of the hospitality we have been offered here in our own capital city in years to come. For it is of such encounters that life-long friendships are forged.

It will be good to hunt again, whether fox, or stag or boar. I know that Ned, too, misses those beasts of his – Satan, most aptly named, and Lysander. I must make a point, at Ménars, of getting Philippe and Aurélien to fit him up with a decent mount.

TOURAINE
1785-86

Versailles, Rambouillet, Chartres, Châteaudun, Vendôme.
Having despatched their own carriage and its attendants back
to England and Grandmamma Fairfax, the Greenwood party
took their leave of the French capital and their friends there,
and set out south-westerly for Chartres, where they were
pause briefly, to view the great cathedral and exchange M. de
Châtigny's carriage for one sent up by M. de Ménars.

Once away from the urban sprawl of Paris and its environs,
as their route took them into the more open terrain beyond
Rambouillet, Julian was aware of an almost tangible
anticipation on the part of the young men of the countryside
and all it would bring with it, the shift of preoccupation, the
different style of dress, the thoughts of particular activities.

"Stag, I think you said, sir?"

"I beg your pardon, Edward?"

"Stag. They hunt stag here."

"They do. And the Val de Loire, the region of the great
river, is particularly given to that kind of thing. The great châteaux
- and some of the not so great - were built expressly with hunting
in view; they are, effectively, hunting lodges. At Chambord, a
king's lodge, there is a vista - deliberately so designed - from
the balcony of the residence which looks straight down the main
avenue of the park to the point at which the hunt ended, so that
the ladies of the King's party who had remained behind could
witness the moment and spectacle of the kill."

"The hunt as spectacle again," said Sebastian.

"Certainly. Do you recall the tapestries at Versailles? Where the point of focus is the King, even as the hounds pull down the stag, which is a mere detail anyway."

"I do, sir, yes. There is a ...concern with ones own self and a preoccupation with gratification, also, which I have to say I find unwholesome."

"Quite so."

"Different from home," said Ned. "At Withybrook we hunt to be rid of the creatures. Foxes, that is. Their ways with the smaller farm animals are not to be tolerated. Apart from that, the fun of the gallop is the point, I'd say."

Julian smiled at the straightforward simplicity of the point; the direct, uncomplicated character of Edward's observations would highlight the more Byzantine aspects of aristocratic antics within their politic sphere.

"True, sir. But what you do need to understand, if I may put it that way, is how the situation of the nobles here *vis-à-vis* the King affects their sense of who they are and of the need to assert their own consequence, or to tell themselves that this is what they are doing, anyway. And those tapestries, in the interest of their makers, flatter the King and those closest to him in just this way. And why do you imagine French kings encourage it so? Hunting, I mean."

"Sir, hunting is... well, hunting, is it not? You make it sound like an act of policy."

"And so it is, Edward, where kings are concerned. Why do you imagine that may be?"

"Because if you are so occupied, you cannot plot?"

"Bravo, Sebastian. Precisely so."

"The life of the *noblesse* here, around the King, seems to me to be one great act of theatre."

"Not inappropriate, sir. You may make a diplomatist, in due course of time. Yes indeed."

"I shall simply hunt for fun, when I am not soldiering," said Edward.

"So you shall, my boy," said Julian, "but I wonder if you appreciate how favoured you are by Fortune, that you should be in a position to say such a thing?"

"I have to allow, sir, that I did not entirely follow your arguments just now, but surely any Englishman is favoured by Fortune? That's what I think, howsoever."

"Quite right, old Ned. Quite right."

"Such pride is an asset, sir. Most decidedly. But, let it remain unassuming. We have no cause or need to enact it in public, wouldn't you say?"

"A point well made, if I may say so, sir," said Sebastian, "and a nice parting comment on Versailles."

"Bearing in mind," said Julian, "that in *milieux* of power it is all too frequently the principles, if that is the right word, of the bully that carry the day. Which does not mean for one moment that one should subscribe to them or compromise oneself where matters involving basic individual honesty are in question. But it is as well to be aware of these things, to know the ways of the world. Castiglione has much to say that is apposite here."

"Castiglione, sir?"

"An Italian cavalry officer of the Renaissance, Edward, who wrote of these matters. With some appropriate English modification, he is well worth the effort."

"Modification?"

"He is a little too inclined to view the monarch, 'the Prince', he would have said, in feudal terms as unconditionally deserving of nothing less than absolute loyalty, no matter what. Since the lesson of the Stuarts a hundred years ago we in England no longer view our sovereign quite so slavishly, I think. Our debt to John Hampden and to other, similar members of the gentry is simply inestimable, and as one of that condition myself I shall be happy to explain that another time, if you will remind me. But one can make allowances for Castiglione, for his other excellences."

"So, the meditations of an Italian cavalry officer, then. How does that appeal, old Ned?"

"Can't read Italian, sorry."

"But in English?"

"If the man was a cavalry officer then I imagine he would be much as any other. How could he not be?"

"Good, Edward. Very good." said Julian, "Circumstances mould men, and the circumstances of cavalry warfare have hardly changed in the intervening time. Neither does political conduct change over much, either. There is always the opposition of consensus on the one hand, and dictate on the other."

They were proceeding now through wide-open countryside; from the windows of the carriage huge vistas of flat, agricultural land were visible, and gradually in the distance the ill-matched spires of what was quite obviously a colossal church building were growing higher every minute.

"Chartres," said Julian Greenwood. "A comfortable, clean *auberge* with which I am familiar, a good dinner and soft, well-made beds. We shall view the cathedral tomorrow, gentlemen, then on to Blois and to the great river itself. *Mon Loyre Gaulois*, as one poet once had it. And it shall become your Loire, too, gentlemen, as it once did mine. For we are here for a considerable period, and there will be hunting, as well as further instruction in the language."

"Something of a respite, then," said Sebastian. "One does need time to take stock of it all. And Ménars, I promise you, Ned, shall be a home from home."

My dearest Isabella, wrote Harriet de Savigny, *Christmas shall soon be upon us, and I spend it this year with my brother and sister-in-law in Hertfordshire. I know they will be happy to entertain my darling Charlotte, who is on the way to becoming a most handsome little lady – you must take the word of her adoring Mamma that this is so! Simon, I think, misses Sebastian more than he allows; he was never really convinced of the value of such a tour as they now undertake, the travelling party, and for an ex-officer who in his campaigning days saw much of the world - both the old and the new - he is curiously without interest in any part of it beyond what comprises his own very modest foothold there. He has of course suffered dreadfully of late in consequence of the wounds he sustained in the American rebellion of ten years ago, and he was never one to take the kind of interest in the affairs and various languages of men which we in the family associate with our Fairfax kinsman, Greenwood, who leads the boys – Sebastian, that is, and his friend Edward Farrell, the Withybrook heir – on their tour. And how one envies them the opportunity of such experience! To travel, to acquire familiarity with the great achievements of the ancient world, to view what remains of its myriad wonderful artefacts, to associate with men of learning, polished manners and worldly wisdom, these are the self-evident advantages of so monumental an undertaking. Yet Simon allowed Sebastian this tour only at my persuasion, and the oaf Withybrook latched on to it merely as a convenient way of ridding himself for a time of an awkward son. Truly, I do despair of our native manners, and the lack of the kind of wisdom that makes for moral grace, even if one has to allow that the wealth and power of England is now something to be marvelled at and reckoned with.*

As Christmas approaches my thoughts shall be with you, my darling Isabella, in your Mediterranean fastness, and once the New Year is here and the early weeks of the January winter over I shall begin my preparations to join you in that heavenly place, with its vistas of 'wine-dark sea'; by which time too no doubt the hibiscus and the bougainvillea will once again be well on the way to adding their gorgeous colours to the scene. Oh, how one longs for the South here, even as the snow, the hunting, the feasts of game and the rich wines which traditionally go with these afford their own particular pleasures. And à propos, my darling Charlotte is to have her first pony, a gift from her ever kind Grandsire Hawkhurst. Eager preparations are afoot in the stables at Hawkhurst Savigny to accommodate the little lady, and to turn her into the elegant mounted one she is to become. I envisage her some ten years hence, painted by one of the fashionable men of the new day, side-saddle, in an elegant habit on an exquisite Arab, in a portrait to hang in one of our greatest houses for generations to come. 'The Honourable Miss de Savigny'! What a pity it is that she cannot succeed to the Hawkhurst title. I am perfectly aware that, much as they adore this little girl, my sweet, kind, loving Lord and Lady Hawkhurst are avid for a son from Peter in order that the name may continue. But not from me, although in my own interest I may not say as much. And I have long since ceased to concern myself with thoughts of Peter, or anything pertaining to his continued existence.

Enjoy your French Christmas, my darling friend. Shall you have a crib of 'santons'? I have always loved the idea, from the old tales of Provence, that the whole village should be represented as present at the birth of the Christ child, in just the same way as we at Hawkhurst Savigny celebrate the event with all the estate folk. So, one should bear witness to the miraculous birth in the company of the butcher, baker, priest and garlic-seller, as well as with the three Kings of Orient and the shepherds, and the players of 'boules', of course, and the pastis drinkers and the card players – always cheating! – and the 'ravi', the village idiot, and the gossips of the place and the huntsmen with their fowling pieces, and the poacher with rabbits in his pockets, and also the esquire and his lady, like Lord and Lady Hawkhurst. For truly it all does add up, all of that, to a proper sense of what that Birth should signify. How one does long to believe that there may be loving consolation for us all somewhere... After the bitter, bitter loneliness of this mortal span, where even the real mitigation, the privilege of ones love as a mother for ones child can afford only temporary and incomplete respite from the world. But, dearest Isabella, it ill behoves me to visit my fit of melancholy upon you, who strives so courageously against that which assails you. And indeed, I count myself fortunate in my circumstances, and should no doubt find a measure of contentment in spite of all, had it not been for what my Prince Charming of Benaco was able to show me of other possibilities at that time of magic. And what an utterly damnable irony, that the sweetest love possible should leave such discontent in its train! For I have to say that I now shy away from opportunities of the heart, in apprehension of their falling short of what I know myself to be capable of , and what I recall still so vividly. In the world of fashion here I am sought after by gentlemen as avid as any savage of the American wilderness for scalps to display about their person. But, being without fortune equal to the unceasing, relentless demands of that world, I fear I have worked myself into a situation of deadly peril, as I have value only as a potential conquest, and nothing more serious than that. So I choose to remain the untouchable Mrs de Savigny, a subject no doubt for the lewd gossip of gentlemen in clubs and coffee-houses.

My dearest friend, I would not burden you with such matters, were it not that you are my only true confidante. I do depend upon your understanding and sympathy so very much more than I can say. Be with me, then, in your thoughts, and soon, very soon, we shall be together again. And may all the blessings of this Christmas Season be yours, my darling...

From the balcony of the villa, colonnaded with its Tuscan arches, Isabella Westlake, cocooned in wool against the chill of the season, gazed out at the historic sea beyond the bright, pantiled roofs of the village below her. The tenderness of Harriet's concern for her was as always; the desolation of spirit in this latest missive had, however, never before made itself so explicit. Isabella found herself this time quite discountenanced by the strength of feeling that her friend, usually so circumspect, had allowed to show through. It was as though Harriet, on an impulse of confidentiality born of remorseless need, had given a clear indication of the true character of a disease which hitherto she had allowed to be taken as no more than slight. And what an irony, that her splendid Harriet - so strong, so vital, so full of resource, so indomitable in all of those her circumstances of which she, Isabella, knew - should suffer so, morally, even as she herself suffered physically from the ailment responsible for her exile.

Isabella Westlake, at thirty years of age, had gradually but inevitably come to terms with the virtual certainty that her life was not to be a long one, as incredulity had given way to resignation, as indeed it usually will. From the splendid promise of her early adult years as a brilliant lady of fortune, she had been cast down effectively without premonition, viciously demoted from heiress to invalid, removed from the delights of elegant society to the solitude of ill-health and dreadful vulnerability. So she learned to cultivate her modest garden in a manner more contemplative, with more to it of rumination than she might have imagined possible in her more active days. And gradually her friends had fallen away, detached themselves quite simply in order that they might continue to pursue their fashionable occasions, for in the clash of such rival compulsions Isabella could only be the loser. Harriet alone, dear, dear Harriet for all her headlong scrapes, had never abandoned her. Isabella knew, without any shadow of doubt, that Harriet would always be there for her; it was something upon which she had come to depend more than she knew, until now. And now, she understood, her friend needed *her.*

Isabella looked out to sea that bright, sunny morning and resolved that she could do no less for her friend than that friend had done, in her way, for her. To fall morally short of equal measure was quite simply unthinkable; now was the chance to reciprocate to some degree, to show her appreciation of the love so freely and undemandingly given by her brilliant, unhappy friend. Isabella could have been jealous of what Harriet had

had - with Fabrizio di Benaco, for instance – that she would now never know, but instead she called for pen, ink and paper and set about her letter in a state of quite unwonted elation. To be of use to Harriet, to be of service... Momentarily all the enforced passivity of her invalid state was forgotten, put aside given the prospect of an active contribution. And thus, in this way, Isabella Westlake drew strength and purpose from the plight of her beloved friend.

MON LOYRE GAULOIS

From Gien in the east to Serrant in the west the magical châteaux of the Loire dream their timeless dreams along the banks of the great river and in the forests of the hinterland to the south. From Chartres via Châteaudun the travellers made their way across the plain to Vendôme and on to Blois via Talcy, where the tiny château built by the Florentine banker, Bernard Salviati, has its unobtrusive, exquisite place in the middle of nowhere, by contrast with the more grandiose, more flamboyant claims of the royal hunting lodges along the south bank of the river itself.

The châteaux, Julian mused, might well make a way into the history of France for the young men; Edward could hardly fail to be impressed by the aristocratic opulence of the great palaces, with their tapestries, furniture, paintings and *objets d'art* - and here, in a moment of memory quite unprompted, Julian recalled the bronzes by Benvenuto Cellini which stand on the chimneypiece at Azay-le-Rideau; Sebastian would be more taken with the literary associations of many of the various residences, of which this tiny, dwelling, Talcy, was, ironically, one of the most potent. For this had been the home of the exquisite Cassandre Salviati, so briefly glimpsed by the tonsured oblate, Pierre de Ronsard, in the torchlight of a ball at Blois, the subject of his marvellous lines in celebration of transient, female beauty. Julian heard them in his head again now, as once he had heard them spoken by an elegant French aunt, now long since dead, who had known what it meant to grow old.

Mignonne, allons voir si la rose,
Qui ce matin avait déclose
Sa robe de pourpre au soleil
A point perdu cette vesprée
Les plis de sa robe pourprée
Et son teint au votre pareil.

Las! Voyez comme en peu d'espace
Elle a dessus la place,
Las! Las! Ses Beautés laisse cheoir!
O vraiment marâtre Nature,
Puisqu'une telle fleur ne dure
Que du matin jusques au soir.

Donc, si vous me croyez, mignonne,
Tandis que votre age fleuronne
En sa plus verte nouveauté, cueillez, cueillez
Votre jeunesse:
Comme à cette fleur, la vieillesse
Fera ternir votre beauté. *

Could one as young as Sebastian, he wondered, appreciate the oblate's sense of 'marâtre Nature', with all that implied of disorder within the order of things? Or the remorseless, irredeemable passing of time, with its rough depredations? Did those classic lines, product of one of the most accomplished literary minds of the day, enact anything more than the wishful lust of one whose rank and circumstances could never allow him to be anything other than an onlooker, a momentary witness to the heart-breaking loveliness of a sweet Italian child-lady viewed by torchlight?

"*Mignonne...*" *my sweet darling...* Could he, Julian, ever convince Edward, say, that verses such as these were worth more to humankind than all the treasures of the Loire châteaux together? For the haunting power of that male perception of

*see p81 for author's translation

female desirability belonged to all the world, not just to the few...In the gathering gloom of the December day, Julian found himself revisited, as invariably, by his old sense of the glory of the region and what it embodied in the way of human achievement – literary, artistic, architectural. Surely the Loire Valley represented one of the great peaks of old world civilisation. And their appreciation of all this should be made to lead them to the Italian Renaissance, to all that Florence, Rome and Venice would have to offer. And yet, though, perhaps tours of this order, so rich in what they had to signify to the human condition, might be better left to later life? Certainly the savour of it all could not but improve with advancing years? A wry thought to entertain, true, but Julian knew the worth of his experience and saw how it would colour and enhance his sense of what they were about; and he was glad to have agreed at last to undertake the tour despite his initial misgivings. How could one have forgotten ones acquired sense of this miraculous region? But it is the immediacy of even the most valued impressions which fades so swiftly. Which is presumably what 'immediacy' is about.

Lost in such rumination, Julian suddenly realised they were now making their way through Blois by the main thoroughfare, as it curved right and down towards the great bridge across the Loire. Once on the far side, they would soon be turning west with the flow of the river, beyond Beauregard, Cheverny, Fougères-sur-Bièvre, towards Montrichard and Amboise, and away from the low-lying, fen-like country of Sologne with its ponds and marshes. And there, in the wooded country between Chenonceaux and Valençay, in its own modest space bracketed by forest, stood the Château de Ménars.

Off the main highway and into the final stretches, landmarks of recollected familiarity begin to appear - a mill-house with its water-wheel by a lazy, winding brook with huge lilies, great green plates, on the surface of the stream, its banks recalled from summer as rich with rushes and weeping-willow – had he fished there, with his young kinsman by marriage, Charles de Ménars, now *châtelain* and *seigneur* of these domains? A calvary on its moss-coloured plinth, a copse of trees of a particular shape, an odd bend in the road. Then he got the next bit wrong, because it was not as he remembered it, or rather, because he had forgotten what had once been so familiar. But there was no mistaking the turn into the entrance to the grounds of the house, past the funny gatehouse and straight up the drive to where, in the gathering gloom of twilight, the old château with its pepper-pot towers at the angles of the frontage and its symmetrical rows of shuttered windows was standing just as it had stood for centuries, but this time as if it awaited them.

The carriage pulled up at the steps to the main entrance, where the door was now opened to allow the soft glow of candles from within to combine with the brash glare of torches from outside, the whole making a pool of fiery light against the darkness of this forest world.

Charles de Ménars, elegant in evening brocade and perruque, silk stockings and buckled shoes, came swiftly down to them, his features animated by the good humour of his welcome to his old friend.

"*Mon cher cousin!*"

"*Charles!*"

The two embraced, shook hands, stood back and eyed one another. Behind Julian, Sebastian and Edward awaited their moment, and as they did so two young men of their own age, similarly attired to their parent, appeared smiling before them. Philippe, the eldest, and Aurélien de Ménars, younger brother and boon companion in scrapes. The English visitors were introduced to the Count, their host, then the brothers hurled themselves at Sebastian, pummelled him enthusiastically and were made known to Edward. At a brisk gesture from M. de Ménars servants appeared to unload trunks and boxes, the party made its way into the panelled hall of the château to where Madame de Ménars and her daughters had gathered. From somewhere towards the rear of the house the rich, gamey odours of country food in preparation were briefly discernible, until a door was quickly closed. And this, for the next months of winter, was to be their home.

By now night had drawn in round the old château, and somewhere in the woods outside an owl hooted. Through a half-open door Edward caught sight of a table glittering with bright glass and silver and realised how hungry he was. He understood also what relief he was feeling to be away from the highway almost indefinitely, with no prospect for the moment of, tomorrow, yet another stretch of their mammoth journey to be undertaken.

So, mindful of the resolutions prompted by his earlier appreciation of the sweet cousin in Paris, Edward, despite his fatigue, found himself responding easily to the friendly welcome proffered by Madame de Ménars and the two bright-eyed little girls beside her, who had quite obviously been allowed to stay up for the occasion and who were, he noticed, eyeing them with considerable interest.

"C'est un milord, Maman?" piped up the elder of the two, only to be smilingly silenced by her mother.

"O, mon pauvre père!" he said, to the delight of Madame de Ménars, who chuckledappreciatively and whispèred a rapid explanation to the girls.

"Monsieur ne devient milord qu'à la mort de son père!"

"Je m'appelle Edward Farrell," he said, *"Edouard, en français. Et vous?"*

"Jeanne de Ménars," said the elder.

"Chantal de Ménars," said the little one.

Totally captivated, Edward bowed gravely to each in turn, and would have gone on to ask them their ages, but the French was beyond him, and as they stood there silent in their mutual appreciation, Madame de Ménars ushered the girls away, leaving Edward to wonder, even as he turned to Sebastian and the older, male cousins, why it might be that he had never understood until now what it might have been like to have had sisters.

At Ménars, under the guidance of Mr Greenwood and with the unflagging help and patient forbearance of the family, Edward Farrell learned to speak more than passable French – very largely because in their present circumstances he simply could not bear to be bettered by Sebastian. School had been one thing; the family here – with dinner or cards, fencing or riding or games about the grounds – was something quite different. And with increasing command, there came the great enjoyment not only of knowing and understanding what was said to him, but of finding oneself in a position to observe, to perceive aspects of character and individuality in others which, without knowledge of their language and idiom, would have been wholly closed off to him.

Jeanne, aged eleven, showed herself to be insatiably curious about his life in England. It did not prove at all easy to pin down and categorise the most significant differences between the two countries, and Edward found himself obliged to begin by convincing the little girl that England was not just another France across the Channel, as it were. And what were the houses like? His house, for instance? Was it like theirs? As big? Or bigger? Surrounded by forest? He was a *milord,* she still insisted, so perhaps he lived in London, as many of the French *noblesse* lived at Versailles? She thought she might rather like to live at Versailles, in a great palace with the King. Edward thought of their visit and shuddered; and he thought of the great, lonely residence in its tailored parkland at Withybrook in Warwickshire, now inhabited only by his parents and their army of retainers. How could he make comparisons between that and the homely wooded domain of the Château de Ménars, so elegantly, unmistakeably aristocratic, with its exquisite, polished Italian furniture and rich tapestries – of the hunt, of battle, of the Court – its silver and fine, Venetian glass and beautifully crafted panelling so lovingly painted and gilded. For Ménars had about it, he and Sebastian had agreed, what Versailles quite definitely did not, an aura of having been lived in, of having simply been there for a long time; its character of distinction had been acquired by virtue of the care and attention of generations of country noblemen to whom it had been home, *la maison,* for the duration of their existences, who had hunted and fished, and learned from childhood the lore of countryside, woodland and river; who had brought their lady brides to the château and bred and brought up their children there, and imparted their knowledge of the place and its ways, of the style and character of the cycle of the seasons, the habits and ways of the creatures as native to the locality as were they themselves. No wonder, Sebastian mused after discussion of stag and boar with Philippe and Aurélien, no wonder they were so knowledgeable, for this was a kind of knowledge imbued from birth, from the moment of the tiny child's first witness of the hunt gathered before the old château, from the first taste of venison, the recollection of an early blooding, all these things had comprised an induction into a way of life which had not changed in its essentials for centuries. And it did briefly occur to Edward that the Withybrook peerage, conferred with the Warwickshire estate by Charles the Second barely one hundred years previously for some manner of equivocal service to the restored monarchy of England was not, after all, so venerable. Although he was, or would be a *milord* when he succeeded. But, be that as it may, he knew and acknowledged that these particular Frenchmen, so unassumingly secure in their rank and station, would never even think to make anything of that one way or another, however self-consciously superior the flunkeys of Versailles might choose to be. For Edward had seen the point of Sebastian's comment on that after his own encounter with one who would never know just how very close he had come to a good English drubbing. And he was led to think of the father who had shown himself so domineering towards his only son, who had always been so *nice* over matters of rank and title, so loudly, apparently sure of his impregnable superiority to a world he held largely in an exhibitionistic, supercilious contempt and which, quite possibly, Edward now understood, did actually assail him with apprehension and uncertainty. And he thought of his Father with impatience and irritation, but also, for the first time, with indulgence rather than fear.

*

Sebastian's diary was growing apace, and as it expanded to accommodate his reflections upon the increasing variety of their experiences since leaving home, so the compulsion grew to work on it, to take in the growing body of material which would eventually comprise the record of his current life-time, he now saw, of the Tour of Foreign Parts. "A Tour of Foreign Parts 1785-86" by Sebastian Haverhill. He sat and eyed that, in the dim light of his candle , with a certain complacency. Of course others had done it before, and very likely in a manner considerably more accomplished than ever he could contrive; but that was not the point, and Sebastian knew it was not. At the rate at which he was composing, the 'Tour' in all seemed likely to fill several volumes – one for France, one for Italy, one for the German lands, perhaps? Once home he would have his diaries bound in leather – or perhaps he would have his text printed first? The volumes would become a part of his private collection and take their place in the library he planned to build with the years, the archive of learned material it was his intention to put together over the course of his life. Sebastian was writing now about his friend.

I have been observing Farrell, he wrote, *from the moment he was first made acquainted with my Uncle Greenwood right up to now, and I have to say that in certain important respects this Tour seems to be proving of considerably greater value to him than it is to me. But I must elaborate upon that, for of course I have already benefited to a very considerable degree from the splendid experiences which have been ours even so far. Paris and the Châtignys and their circle – such polish and wit, and knowledge both learned and worldly, and so lightly worn! Maître Courtois, a true savant of the blade such as one could never have dreamed existed, in whose sense of the possibilities of the weapon there was a logic and clarity almost philosophical; Versailles and the huge banality of power and vainglory; Chartres and the power of medieval piety to build so awe-inspiring an edifice; Talcy and the Ronsard association... the list becomes longer and longer.*

Also, I have begun the kind of idiomatic fluency of speech in the French tongue which I have observed and envied in my Uncle Greenwood's discourse in that language, and which is something, I understand, which may come about only in consequence of an extended sojourn among those indigenous to the country in question. Ned, too, is beginning to speak more confidently than one might have imagined possible when one recalls his total lack of interest at Westminster. But here lies the point in question: Ned learns to speak to cope with particular situations. He began to make the effort in Paris because he wished to engage the interest of his cousin, Clothilde; here he is compelled to speak because the little girls, Jeanne and Chantal, insist he does so without, I surmise, any sense at all of the difficulty of what is involved. When he talks hunting or swordplay with Philippe or Aurélien the conversation centres upon necessary technicalities, matters of strictly practical moment – how best to riposte from a parry in quinte, *what the style might be of the boar's flight from hounds, whether one might compare fox and boar in this regard, and if not, why not. Lord Withybrook, I know, agreed to this Tour to be rid of an awkward son, to be free of any report of yet more 'scrapes' for at least a while, and nothing more. So it is quite unwittingly then that he has done the old Ned the most signal of favours. For the spiky pugilist of our schooldays with his 'Do you mock me, man?', his idiot punctilio – no doubt acquired from the appalling parent, who else? – over rank and title have been much less in evidence of late. This is as a result of our continued proximity to such as the Châtignys and the Ménars; it is also one consequence of dear old Nedward's terrific sentimental susceptibility to the charms of ladies, of whatever age. Oh, for some means of recording the sight of the Honourable Ned explaining to that bright little lady, Jeanne de Ménars, how to prime a fowling piece! As if she really wished to know anything more of that than she probably already does! But her "Edouard!", or "Monsieur Edouard!" when within earshot of her Mamma or Papa. "Que faites-vous?" "Montrez-moi!" will ring happily in our ears for ever, I think, when we recall this time from our later years. The sound of their speech, for instance, the little girls, the sweetness of their enunciation is of such loveliness as it rings upon the ear. And cousin Sophie, Madame de Ménars, knows just how to make allowances for our difficulties and hesitations in speech, our frantic quests for the 'mot juste'.*

One is so at home here, much as the grander moments have been appreciated – the acquaintances all too briefly encountered through the Châtigny family; Versailles, of which more shortly; the visit to Chartres, brief but long enough to leave an impression of some significance; the great châteaux here – we have already seen Chambord and Azay-le-Rideau... As Christmas approaches we know it will be all one could hope for, both as a religious celebration – we are of course to witness the Catholic rite this year – and the more homely aspects of the festival at the château. This will be the high point in this first stage of our tour, and one to crown – or at least to epitomise in highlight these idyllic months away from the road. Then, with spring, we are eventually to make for the great routes to the South, most likely across to Bourges , then Moulins, and Lyons, and on possibly even down the great river Rhône as far as Avignon. One longs for this, of course, even as one appreciates how difficult it will surely be to take our leave of these kindly cousins who have so readily taken us into their family circle and made us of their number.

Tomorrow at first light we hunt. Friends will be joining us: the Montrichard wine people from Gièvre, the seigneur and his guests from Beauregard, back up by Blois, others not yet known to us. One of the most interesting aspects of a sojourn in this region is to be found in what one learns of the smaller châteaux, as well as of the great and famous ones renowned far and wide. Of course Chambord is splendid – deservedly so with that wonderful roof-top village of towers and streets and alleyways, where those not hunting could amuse themselves with their games and flirtations and assignations – oh, to pleasure a lady in bright sunshine on the roof-top of a fine palace! Amboise, too, is splendid with its associations of Leonardo - what a time that must have been, when the Kings of France could command such power and influence! The evidence of Renaissance genius in such places – those Cellini bronzes at Azay, for instance – is overwhelming. And indeed, the treasures of mind, art and manufacture here are almost too much to comprehend, given the glut of excellence in so many forms wherever one may choose to turn.

The smaller châteaux here – Talcy, Beauregard, Ménars among them – assert their consequence more modestly but with an equal claim to regard, and in consideration of this one cannot but conclude that the unassuming character of their claims is as much if not more to be esteemed for its own understated, mannerly style than the more flamboyant and ostentatious displays of the great royal residences of the neighbourhood.

For in the great world of power and prestige, the magical paintings, the exquisite, Italian furniture, the rich tapestries of country and Court life mythical or actual, the glassware from Venice, the porcelain from Sevres so delicately and lovingly crafted, all these things are there, one feels, not as examples of what is best achieved by the finest of our kind. For artists and craftsmen are certainly *not conventionally perceived as such, and decidedly not by kings and men of power who perceive only themselves and their own exclusive concerns – but as symbols of wealth and status, reminders, badges even, of power and predominance which exist, not in their own right as things exquisite and admirable for what they represent in the way of the best capabilities of the most gifted men, but to enforce an awesome if unpalatable truth about consequence and domination. There is undoubtedly a kind of corruption at the heart of the great world, where the grandees of those heady reaches play out their deadly games, and you may literally stake your life on a manoeuvre or stratagem in the full knowledge that death or humiliation, both conceivably hideous, may well be the penalty for an unfortunate turn of events, or a miscalculation however slight in itself. But it is equally clear that there is an exhilaration to be had from it all, just as in gaming the element of risk becomes addictive.*

One cannot but enquire, however, setting the king against the philosopher, which of these two it is makes the most enduring contribution to the well-being of his fellow men. And looking at the great French thinkers – philosophers and poets of the last two hundred years – one cannot but conclude that they have done rather better than the Bourbons. So I choose the way of the philosopher, mine shall be the contribution of a scholar and, perhaps even in due course, a savant. Had I been a military man like my Father I might have chosen, unlike him, to go for the high honours of rank and distinction, although without access to the kind of influence that – may God help us all! – Farrell wields, I would undoubtedly have had a greater chance in His Majesty's Navy. But I am none, and it is as a philosopher , then, that I shall hope to make some kind of mark. And even as I pen these thoughts, I must allow in all honesty that I am not unaware of the irony of my position. For influence over the minds of men is nothing less than an alternative form of power, to which the Roman Church bears eloquent witness. And as such, can it be any more acceptable than the other kind? Can there be no honourable way, in endeavour of any kind, of avoiding this impasse? Urged and argued perhaps, rather than enforced, a view may become acceptable to the judicious. For one cannot rightly, morally compel belief or acquiescence, however much it may be the way of the bullying world to do so.

But that is not the ideal, the Greek way as I understand that. I shall look forward to a perusal of recent German deliberations on these matters, but they shall be for when that time comes. We have still so much ahead of us.

To Cassandra   Pierre de Ronsard

My sweet darling, let us go and see
If the rose which this morning
Displayed her crimson gown to the sun
Has this evening lost anything
Of those gorgeous pleats,
Or of her blush like yours.

Alas, my darling, see how briefly
She keeps her superior state!
Alas, for such beauty fallen low!
And oh, marauding nature, in truth,
If such a bloom as this may last
Only from dawn to dusk.

So, my sweet, if you will take my word,
Make the most of your young life
As it burgeons now so fresh and green.
For old age will have your loveliness fade,
As it has had that of the rose.

THE SOUTH
Spring 1786

In mid-March, as the Loire weather became softer and brighter, the travelling party moved on southwards, having insisted on promises from the Ménars scions that they would one day make the journey to England, where exchange of languages would continue and hospitality be returned.

"Un de ces jours, Mesdemoiselles, vous viendrez me visiter en Angleterre, vous me le promettez?" Edward had asked.

Gravely proper in the formality of their leave-taking, the two little girls, Jeanne and Chantal, had at last thrown caution to the winds and hurled themselves at Sebastian and Edward who, Julian observed, had been equally moved by the poignancy of the moment. Between the young men, things had been somewhat brusquer and more laconic.

"Foxes in Leicestershire then, in a year or two's time?"

"Certainly, Edouard", Philippe had said, "we shall look forward to it."

Then they had turned away, leaving the group of kindly, generous friends to watch from the steps of the château as their carriage made its way down the drive and through the gated entrance-way by the lodge, where it turned left and was lost to view. And all too soon even the sound of its progress faded into silence, a silence which, to Sophie and Charles de Ménars and their children had been weighted with their sense of regret, and of the sorrow invariably attendant upon the parting of friends.

Bourges, Moulins, Lyons, Avignon – such was the planned

route to the South. And where, exactly, did the South, *le Midi,* begin? Julian pondered the matter as they made their way over the early stages of the Sévigné route, digressing for a moment in his thoughts to consider the situation of the lonely marchioness as she had cherished, some hundred years previously, her fond love of a not so loving daughter along the highways from Vitré to Grignan and back. But... boundaries. Where did the South begin? Certainly on mainland Europe mountains came into it, as they defined limits in very obvious ways. *'Beyond the mountains...'* the story-teller's cliché for a notion of 'elsewhere'. And Italy, their present destination for the rest of this year, was certainly inaccessible unless by mountain pass or sea journey, a country virtually cut off from the rest of Europe – apart from the Istrian peninsula – by formidable ranges of snow-clad peaks, whether glittering and dazzling in an altogether brighter sunlight than that of home, or louring through the mist and fog of less hospitable seasons.

Here too, in France, the Massif Central all but barred the way to the southern sea, the only ways through being by winding tracks of hideous tedium round rock and through forest – sometimes, admittedly, of positively epic spectacle and grandiose vista.

So, one went by the Rhône, the second of the great rivers, as far as Avignon – from whence one might well proceed eventually to Nice or thereabouts, before taking ship for Genoa, or destinations along the coast of Liguria. And the anticipation of that lifted Julian's heart, despite his private regret over the parting from cousins he loved, and the children who had come to represent so proud a continuation of the line whose blood, through his cousin Sophie, he shared. But Italy, truly, however multifarious, however memorable the other experiences of the Tour, was quite rightly the centrepiece and focus of such an enterprise, and what lay in store for the young men in Florence, Sienna, Rome, Naples and Venice was quite simply of such unimaginable richness that it could hardly have been otherwise. To consider the connections of the Loire châteaux with the

Renaissance in Florence, for instance... to consider the Renaissance in Italy itself – in Florence, then Rome, and Venice, to imbibe an Italian landscape at sunset, with umbrella pines in silhouette, hill-top citadels and villas of gorgeous historicity – is to ingest the very essence of all that makes for true civilisation, the European civilisation of man-made splendours against that glorious back-drop of mountain, lake, river and forest. And perhaps, for a man of culture and learning such as Julian unassumingly and unsentimentally knew himself -privately- to be, that was where the notion of 'the South' fell most clearly into focus. It comprised those regions where the still living presence of the antique past – of 'Rome', principally, but also of the Greece of ancient time living on both in itself and through its Roman metamorphosis – made itself most immediately apparent. In Provence, for instance, to which they would soon be making their way, the shape of a wine jug, a common, everyday, household utensil, could evoke most vividly the sense of a Rome still very much alive in the thew and sinew of ordinary, humdrum existence.

So far as it is possible to find a sensible, reasonable answer to the question, Julian thought, that answer may have to do with cooking in olive oil from the frugal terrains where goats pick their nimble way, and gnarled, spectacular, twisted trees find means of sustenance and growth in rocky, sun-baked, barely hospitable ground. It may also have to do, as formerly it did, with language – with French as opposed to the *langue d'oc* of Provence. But most significantly, he concluded, 'the South' comprises those regions within reach of the Mediterranean where the presence of Rome – whether in wine jugs, roof-tiles, garden furniture of mosaic patterning framed in wrought iron –is still to be discerned. And *à propos,* Julian understood that his young men had by now accustomed themselves to the initial unfamiliarity of France, of the French scene and French manners by contrast with their own Anglo-Saxon modes, but there were degrees of difference, and they would soon find themselves plunged yet again into an everyday world which operated according to conditions – of climate, temperature, manners and culture – even more alien than that to which they had already adjusted so successfully.

Julian was proud of the way in which both boys had comported themselves over the course of their stay with his Ménars cousins. He had noted the idiomatic ease with which Edward Farrell, the 'bruiser' of previous notoriety, had taken his affectionate leave of Jeanne and Chantal de Ménars. The Honourable Ned, with his 'Do you mock me, man?', and spiky, horrid Withybrook punctilio, was in process of significant development and change, and Julian was not displeased to be the agent of that. And over their time at Ménars Sebastian, too, had hunted, fenced with the brothers and amused the little girls with card tricks and the rare variety of games hundreds of years old which had been passed down from one generation to the next within Charles's family. There had been one which he recollected particularly from his own earlier times there, where a wooden ball of roughly cannon-ball dimensions, embossed with brass – or iron? – knobbed protuberances had to be rolled into a hole of commensurate size at the centre of a table presumably specially constructed for the purpose ages previously, since the wood was white, cracked and dry with age. The young people had spent hours at this, invaluable hours for the Englishmen, since they had acquired language almost without realising it. And Julian had spent long hours in conversation with his old friend and cousin – as the French so graciously have it – Charles de Ménars, a man steeped in knowledge of his beloved France and its civilisation.

And during the course of those long winter evenings too there had frequently been stories read or recounted in the soft candlelight of the *salon*. Julian thought again of the magical voice of his cousin, Sophia Fairfax, Sophie de Ménars, as she read to her daughters. *'Il y avait, une fois...'* that voice, speaking a French which was quite simply beyond, way beyond perfection, had compelled the attention of everyone within earshot. Whatever else you might be engaged with, you stopped to listen to Madame la Comtesse as she read.

Now though that stage of the Tour was behind them, and the whole of the next twelve months or so would see them first in Provence, where they would enjoy the Roman ruins of Nîmes, Arles and Vaison-la-Romaine, and acquaint themselves with the wines of Gigondas, Vacqueyras and Baumes de Venise and possibly, it now occurred to him, make the walk to the bare, forbidding summit of Mont Ventoux. Three or four days of highway travel should not prove too onerous, once one had steeled oneself to the thought that they were once again *en route*. They could be comfortable overnight, he knew, in Bourges and Lyons. The advantage of the larger towns was that there was usually decent lodging to be had, and this time, too, they would be close enough to the great vineyards of Burgundy to sample some of the truly great labels and vintages. Travel may bring its particular discomforts in its train, but it did also have its very decided compensations.

And then, Provence. They were to lodge, by courtesy of Charles de Ménars, in private rooms of their own close by the exquisite Place d'Albertas in the old quarter of Aix-en-Provence, an elegant, sun-lit town with its splendid avenues of plane trees which Julian remembered with affection from his brief sojourn at the university there.

In Provence, too, they were to make a start on the Latin and historical studies of the legacy of the ancient world and of Rome in particular. This would be anew addition to the programme, for they were to continue with their French and make a something of a start on the Italian language before they did actually arrive in that country. Where Germany was concerned... they should get by on their French, which was in any event the language of polite society in those lands. Julian was certain that Sebastian would one day wish to embark on a thorough study of the German tongue for himself; he had already spoken of his desire to read the savants of their own century, indeed of their own time, in their own language. But a continued interest in spoken French, together with a look at the rudiments of Italian and the Latin reading that he, Julian, had insisted they work upon would be more than enough over the two years of their time abroad. Anything more would, as he understood the matter, be an infliction, and one which might easily mar the pleasure of their recollections of the Tour in years to come.

By now the colossal medieval silhouette of the great Gothic cathedral of Bourges had loomed into view, a distant focus across the huge, flat vista of the plain over which they were now travelling. Julian hailed Charles de Ménars' coachman to halt briefly; they were to step down and take in this extraordinary sight. The young men did as they were bidden, staggered, stretched and considered the prospect.

"A constant, visible presence," said Sebastian.

"Sebastian?"

"The Church, sir. The Roman Church. It manifests its presence constantly, in the most obvious, most obtrusive and intrusive ways."

"Certainly it does. And by design. Although amongst enlightened people - and I use the term deliberately – it no longer has the hold it once enjoyed, under Louis XIV for instance. The climate of this, our time here in France is not with the Church as it was a century ago."

"And yet, the same family still rules the land."

"True. But personalities do not replicate themselves, sir. The Sun King was a man of unique stature. His posterity has not contrived to match him. And besides, he merely held up, in France, what was already on the move elsewhere in the north of Europe. Consider our own Restoration, the founding of the Royal Society, Isaac Newton, our 'revolution' of all but one hundred years ago, the writings of Mr Locke. We are a century ahead of France in these things. And where we accommodate those dissident minds which frequently constitute the sources of innovation and change, they suppress theirs. Why do you imagine M. de Voltaire lives so close to the Swiss border?"

"To make a run for it, when the going gets rough?"

"Edward, I could not have put it better myself. That is precisely what he does."

"Then who publishes him, sir?"

"The Swiss, or the Dutch. The latter particularly, I think. The enlightened countries do tend to be of republican persuasion, in their politics. Or, if they are monarchies, of the constitutional kind."

"Sir?"

"Where the king rules, Edward, with the consent of his Parliament. Do you recall the name of John Hampden, gentlemen? When King Charles I demanded payment of a new tax without reference to the Commons, Mr Hampden – and others like him – refused to pay it. In England, of course, the case of John Hampden, Gentleman was the beginning of the end for the kind of absolute monarchy the Stuarts stood for. The fact that the Bourbons still do should give cause for concern - in my view, and that of friends, they are heading for trouble, in this year of Our Lord 1786."

"M. de Ménars? M. de Châtigny?"

"Both, Sebastian. Both. Shall we be on our way?"

For the north European, the Anglo-Saxon especially, perhaps, it is easy to believe that the South begins at the Loire, for the climate is distinctly milder there, the warmth of the sun more assertive, the advance of the warm seasons earlier than in the regions of the North. But this is to reckon without the further changes of degree to which conditions are subject as one makes the laborious journey across huge tracts of central France. There are compensations of course for the tedium of the in-between. Soon, it is clear, the golden vineyards of Burgundy will appear, bathed in the kind of sun-lit glow that nurtures and cajoles the great vintages into their miraculous fruition; here it is warmer, more welcoming even, than the Val de Loire. And some degrees of latitude more and the sun will blaze, and the natives avoid it.

So the travellers wend their way steadily southwards; at

this stage of their journey there is nothing for it but to endure, with kind of forbearance that is the hallmark of the true adventurer.

Bourges - Moulins - Macon - Lyons. And the Roman regions of Provence, the great *Provincia* of antiquity draw closer day by day.

At Macon they ordered wine to be despatched home to England; from there they had pursued their route due south to Lyons, where they had lodged and dined in some style, and where the young men had had their first taste of *aioli,* the garlic mayonnaise of Provence. A positively splendid Condrieu from Vienne had evoked real appreciation not untouched by some amazement on Edward's part.

"We pass that way tomorrow, Edward. Why not send your Father some?"

"I shall, sir. And I shall have him put some by for me. I have to say, I should never have believed it."

"Well, now you know better, Farrell, do you not?"

"Most decidedly. But have you drunk this before, Sebastian? Surely not?"

"*Mais si!* As they so conveniently say here. At my Uncle Greenwood's up in Lancashire."

"How extraordinary! Oh, I do beg your pardon, sir!"

"My dear boy, please! But I do believe I still a have a dozen or two. And now is as good a time as any, indeed better than most, to despatch a few more to keep them company. I had quite forgotten, I must allow, how very special this is. But let us now have words with the *sommelier* over something rather nice in the red line. A Burgundy, of course. A bottle or two, don't you think?"

That night Edward dozed, pondered and eventually dreamed. It was as if the glow of contentment induced by excellent and exceptional wines had suddenly come to epitomize, as it were, the happiness and success of the first, French phase of their Tour so far. He saw himself back in England, quietly confident over wine and swordplay, imagined himself in portrait as a cornet of Life Guards, hand on sword, head proudly high.

At Ménars there had been such a portrait of Charles, Comte de Ménars, painted, so he had learned from his host, by one Pompeo Batoni, an Italian portrait artist much sought after by the aristocracies of Germany, England and elsewhere. Edward understood from Julian Greenwood that the man, although now of advanced age, might still be disposed to execute such a work, if adequately persuaded.

"You might have him do your head and hands, Edward", Julian had suggested, "the rest can be added in London easily. There are all sorts of fellows of the jobbing kind who could add you a Life Guards' uniform, in due course."

"Unless you end up in the Blues, obviously," said Sebastian.

"One does not *end up* in the Blues, my dear Haverhill," said Edward loftily, as Sebastian stood by, chortling. "But that I shall certainly do, sir. For my parents' house in town, I think. And you shall both view it, and be my guests, and my thanks to you, sir, for the suggestion."

"As long as you do not expect us to *admire* it", said Sebastian.

"We shall most certainly admire whatever there may be about it to be admired," said Julian. Edward grinned.

"I shall refrain from further comment, sir," he had said.

So Edward had dozed happily off to sleep and dreamed a dream of apocalyptic horror, in which the Château de Ménars had gone up in flames, the Count's Batoni been torn from its exquisite gilt frame and ripped to shreds by rough, vengeful, spoiling hands and the family annihilated, as Charles de Ménars and his two sons, sword in hand, had fought a struggle to the death on the steps of their home, to defend it and their sweet and precious ladies against this faceless threat of murder and violation. Edward had started up aghast, his heart pounding.

What could conceivably have prompted all that, a nightmare of the worst possible kind? It was as if the happiness and content of their companionship so far, crowned by the convivial evening they had just spent at the table together, must needs be counter-balanced by an entirely random apprehension of worst contingency. One was, of course, subject to visitations of acute anxiety, most usually in the kind of situation, or plight even, which might give rise to them. The night before his bout with Sid Venus, the Penge Mangler, Edward had lain awake through the small hours wondering just exactly who he was, the Honourable Edward Farrell, fifth Earl of Withybrook one day to be. Added to which there had been a crucial rider, in the form of the very real query whether he would be at all capable of similar thoughts on the morrow, or indeed ever again. So it must be for a duellist, he had mused, facing the prospect of a trial of arms to deadly conclusion. But this nightmare of a Ménars conflagration had been something more random, seemingly, with neither rhyme nor reason to it. Deeply disturbed, Edward had put the memory from his mind. Nor did he say anything of it to his friends. And he was not to recall it for a number of years.

From Lyons the next day they continued on their way down the east bank of the great River Rhône via Vienne, where the Condrieu was duly purchased, then on to Valence and Montélimar after which, the following day, there was a brief detour to view the château at Grignan, home of Françoise de Grignan, daughter of the lonely marchioness de Sévigné who had died there. They had effectively completed the journey, not quite from Brittany to Provence but very nearly, conceived by Julian back at the Hôtel de Châtigny in Paris, when he had mused over the exquisite letters of the widowed marchioness pining for her beloved daughter, with a husband, Henri de Sévigné, despatched in a duel at the age of twenty-five, and a son, Charles, a feckless, foolish heir who had sold off a beloved forest, most likely to defray gambling debts.

As Julian explained all this to the young men, Sebastian was put in mind of Peter de Savigny, and wondered briefly where Harriet was, and whether they might see her again soon. But in Aix-en-Provence anyway there would be opportunities... he and Edward had already decided, in terms of the tacit code of exchange which had grown up between them over the years of their friendship, that a sojourn of some length in a town of some size would certainly afford intimations and opportunities of adventure and delight. For, if one may not importune ones lady cousins, there do exist others of that sex whose business and pleasure it is to make themselves rather more available... The prospect of languid, drowsy afternoons in enjoyment of good-humoured, expert ministrations accompanied by inconsequential exchanges of utterly casual discourse were greatly to be relished. At Ménars, before they had left, Philippe and Aurélien had passed on one or two addresses, certain names... Clearly, the pied-à-terre in Aix had its variety of uses.

And so, at last, to Provence. From Grignan, perched in all its Renaissance splendour on its outcrop of rock high above the plain to the south, they turned back to the river , to travel by that route as far as the great walled stronghold-city of Avignon, skirting Orange *en route,* with Mont Ventoux prominent in the background to the east, and Carpentras not far removed.

And the colours of landscape, sky and dwelling – from the grandest to the most humble – assaulted Sebastian's memory and lodged themselves there for ever, so that all his subsequent life he would recollect the brilliance of the typical, bright orange, Roman-style roof-tiles against the intense azure of a sky from which the sun blazed down unremittingly from dawn to dusk, the dazzling white of the ubiquitous rock, the greens of cypress and umbrella-pine. Certainly there were no paintings with which he was familiar that had done anything like justice to the sheer luminosity of the scene. But for all the foreign unfamiliarity of the region with its myriad towns heaped crazily, higgledy-piggledy about the hill-tops which abounded between the fringes of the Cévennes and the foothills of the great Alpine chain there was, too, a very definite sense of *déjà vu* to the alien splendour of it all. How could this be? Sebastian discussed the matter with Mr Greenwood, who for once had no ready answer.

"I have no ready answer for you, sir, except to say that I, too, sense this and have always done so. Not simply by virtue of having previously visited these parts – to which there is, would you not agree, a very particular character? But consider: there is, for instance, a huge body of popular local folklore with which all are acquainted, from the *seigneur* in his castle to the peasant in his humble dwelling. Provence, quite clearly, does belong to France – the Comte de Grignan, who married Françoise de Sévigné, was after all the King's Lieutenant Governor of the province – but it does differ, even as it belongs, by virtue of its own very strong sense of a distinctive and unique identity. And there is the language, *Occitan,* for instance. Although everyone speaks French as well, and moves easily from the one to the other and back. As far as we are concerned, perhaps despite our Anglo-Saxon origins, the element of Rome may play a part? The presence of Rome still alive, as it were, in the most commonplace things? Or the timeless character of life close to the earth which has been the way of things in Europe since the first settlements? Inaccessible languages can and do impart a superficial sense of alienation, but behind the most outlandish usage there is invariably a common humanity, I think, and with that perhaps a common memory? The patterns of human purpose are usually tediously similar, wherever one may venture. Consider the massive style of this city wall before us, gentlemen. Does it not speak to us of things already known almost from time immemorial? And the scale on which the Palace of the Popes was conceived? Consider the description 'palace' in the first place. It tells us something, does it not? Something we have always known? That the mighty aspire to the condition of the king – because kings live in palaces – and that physical size conveys a notion of commensurate power. These are the things we know. Even if we do not always wish to accept that they are so. The legends and fairy-tales of this part of France have their own fascination, too, where these matters are in question. Regrettably, there are few printed collections, if indeed any, but we might keep our eyes open, gentlemen, don't you think?"

"For tales concocted by the peasantry, sir?"

"Do you imagine then, Edward, that the great and powerful are wiser in the ordinary things of life than those of more humble station? You remember your own stable-boy."

"I must allow, sir, that I have always assumed it to be thus. But listening to you, if you will permit me to say, I frequently find such certainties... called into question, if indeed not contradicted. Forgive me."

"No, no, my dear boy. I have to say that the honesty of your reply delights me. And you will learn, sir, to build a private wisdom upon that kind of uncertainty, and it shall enhance your moral standing as a gentleman of consequence, which is what one would wish for you both. To put it somewhat differently, your words of command as an officer to the men who serve under you will bear more weight with those men – whatever others may insist to you, Edward - if they sense some kind of common ground with you despite the difference in rank and station. And if you require a military precedent, sir, consider Julius Caesar."

"Julius Caesar, sir?"

"Who drank and joked with his men in their own language," added Sebastian, "and told them stories of a kind one can easily imagine, I think, and contrived to suggest decidedly improper things with carrots."

"All of which might be said to add up to something or other, don't you think?"

"And I never realised there were things like that in Caesar!" said Edward,

"I am silenced, sir."

"No, no, my dear boy. That was not my intention at all, not something I should have wished for one moment. You will need to show yourself dutiful and unquestioning to your military superiors, but among friends and equals you should stand your ground and argue your case. For there is nothing more constructive than argument, discussion, qualification and negotiation."

"Perhaps we might look out for some of those old tales you mentioned, sir?"

"Certainly, Sebastian. Who knows what we might come upon, if we comb the booksellers' stocks assiduously enough? We have Avignon before us, and Nîmes, Arles, Aix, Vaison-la-Romaine. We have as a good a chance as any man alive of coming across something of interest."

And duly, in an antiquaire in the old quarter of Aix-en-Provence, no more than minutes from the Ménars pied-a-terre and the Place d'Albertas, they found a dog-eared volume of exquisite *contes,* of a kind more usually passed on down the generations by word of mouth. And there was one in particular which they all found especially pleasing, such that, over their future months of travel, it came to be frequently referred to.

"But, what can we call it?" asked Sebastian. "*Coulobre* is presumably a local rendering of *couleuvre,* wouldn't you say?"

Edward and Mr Greenwood agreed that it most probably was.

"And where, then, does that lead us, exactly?" Sebastian went on.

They all agreed that it did not lead them very far.

"Either," said Sebastian, "we say 'snake', or something similar, like 'monster', or 'dragon', or we coin our own English version of *coulobre.* Say, for instance."

"There may be an alternative", said Mr Greenwood.

"Yes?" said both young men simultaneously.

"In certain of our older poets," said Mr Greenwood, "one finds the word 'worm' used to describe giant, slithery things that hang from the branches of trees in dense forests and ambush unsuspecting knights and officers of the Guards."

Edward snorted into a glass of white wine, choked, coughed then shortly recovered. "A giant worm," he said.

"That's it," said Sebastian. "My compliments, gentleman both."

So, The Bishop and the Giant Worm it was, and after they had finished the bottle between them they took a further look at the tale, which goes as follows:

The Bishop and the Giant Worm

Some distance from Avignon, just in the foothills of the Vaucluse Mountains, there is spring called La Sorgue. It wells up at the foot of a gigantic cliff from an open gash in the soft limestone, and gives birth to the delightful. Wayward river that takes its name from it.

Before the era of civilisation arrived there, the banks of the Sorgue were memorably wild. Above the swift-flowing waters a luxuriant foliage of boxwood and creeper formed a vault both sombre and chill which was not typical of Provence at all. At the foot of the cliff there suddenly opened up a yawning gulf, the darkness of which was quite fearsome. You can make your way in there when the spring is at the level of the lowest water, and you can discern the entrance to two vast caverns, one of them more than sixty feet in height, the other some one hundred feet across and nearly as deep. At the very centre of this gulf there rises the source of La Sorgue.

At its lowest the water, silent and smooth, fills an oval basin, and the over-flow runs out through crevices in the rock which channel it back to the river bed some distance downstream. But after the heavy rains of spring and autumn the water rises inexorably to take over all the space of the rocky shelter, then suddenly it crashes over moss-covered boulders and the stumps of trees, carrying all away with it. The wave overflows in all directions and covers the banks in foam. The waters become calmer only much further downstream, when there are no further obstacles to impede them. Between the cliff and the town which grew up there, like a cluster of water-lilies, the Sorgue regularly unleashes its fury. And the mountains which enclose it on three sides echo the thunder of its cascades until they become deafening. But even more impressive are the massive rocks which, huge and precarious, hang between earth and sky at the side of the cliff, held in place, it seems, only by roots of rosemary and juniper. From time to time one of these will break free from its uncomfortable seat, taking huge clouds of blinding dust with it as it bounces horribly down to the river bed, transforming it for a moment into a geyser.

The country folk will tell you that the top of the cliff is known as the Vache d'Or, *the Golden Cow, and the mountain contains within it a cache of ingots of that precious metal, all guarded by a jealous spirit which remains invisible but which groans lugubriously and lets out hideous cries if anyone is bold enough to approach the cave. Since even the most intrepid are filled with terror there, the treasure remains intact. Once, it is said, the English offered to buy the mountain with its golden contents, but wisely the locals refused to allow this. For a very long time the people of Provence tried to find out where the water came from, for the fountain was one of the most powerful in the world. Shepherds would drop sticks deep into the many crevices of the mountain of Lure, and years later these would be cast up undigested by the river. But the underground current which had borne them away remained unknown, and the mysterious fluctuations in the flow of the fountain were attributed to supernatural causes.*

This was the world in which Saint Véran, Bishop of Cavaillon, took refuge for a time as a hermit. The good monk strode the banks of the Sorgue, refusing the huts offered him and installing himself in a hollow of rock shielded from outside by the sound of the water-falls and the over-arching foliage.

But there still lived in these wild places gods of ancient time, driven from the towns and the countryside, which found shelter only in the subterranean reaches of the mountains and the thickets of the forest. And when the Bishop made his appearance there the whole place was thrown into a state of agitation.

Then, from the abyss of the Sorgue, there emerged a gigantic water-dragon bristling with scaly spikes, its giant wings as sharp and keen as the fins of the scorpion fish. This was the notorious 'Giant Worm', dreaded by all for miles around.

And as he watched Saint Véran was not at all sure of himself despite his saintliness; and the creature began to make the effort to come out from its lair. But it was so gross that it found itself impeded by its own bulk when, roaring and snorting in hideous style, it attempted to bite the Bishop, who now found himself hemmed in against his rock. The monster snapped its jaws, stabbed with its tongue, used its triple teeth to bite with, and all the time lashed the water with a tail needle-sharp along its edges. But its efforts availed it nothing, for Veran leaped to one side as it attacked, feigned flight, accomplished passes which would have made the best of matadors jealous. With his sprinkler in one hand and a chain of iron in the other, he confronted the dragon, danced around its snout, climbed the rock, slipped by the dead tree and came back out right under its nose. The worm, less agile for all its ferocity, was unable to match the Bishop in movement, until eventually, covered in mud, it ended up stuck in the basin of the fountain, whilst its jaws slammed shut high above the huts of the abandoned village. And at last Saint Véran managed to lasso the monster with his iron chain, which he pulled tight with all his strength. And with every twist and turn the worm made to free itself, the knot drew tighter and tighter. It struggled for ages, its side heaving with the effort to keep on breathing; the rocks round about were *smashed to pieces as it desperately tried to get a grip on the nearby oak trees, and as its claws sank deeper into the mud and its tail brought down the walls of the cave where the Sorgue was already turning green with its blood. But Véran still had strength to spare. Thus, overcome, the monster was brought to the plain of Cavaillon then dragged into the ravines of the Luberon, where it was abandoned, half-dead, flat out on the ground, with its head in Lourmarin and its tail at Bonnieux, its last paroxysms ploughing out the folds of the valley terrain by which these two villages are linked today.*

Saint Véran returned to the banks of the Sorgue, cleaned up something of the disorder caused by that mighty conflict, and set himself up peacefully in the demon's cave. The river flowed back into its usual course, and soon the valley was covered with homely flowers. Roses bloomed on their bushes, and the wild cherries grew plump and fat. Along the bare face of the cliff, where hawthorn blossomed and wallflowers flourished, the only sound was that of the Bishop at prayer.

But in the Luberon strange things were happening, for the mountain seemed to be moving. From Gordes and Roussillon you could see the cedars shaking and the flocks in flight. In the Calavon Valley the people of Lacoste, Bonnieux, Auribeau and Castellet had also fled.

For the Giant Worm had not died of its wounds. Having regained its strength, it succeeded in freeing itself from the chain of iron which had shackled it to the tower of the Saint Symphorien priory, and heaved up a body wracked with pain, bruised and damaged all over but still living. It shook itself, stretched, gave vent to hoarse cries which shook the mountain and terrorised the countryside as far as Venaissin, stood itself painfully upright and, pointing itself at the horizon, with a last effort which occasioned a complete collapse of the rock quarry at Espeil, took ponderous flight.

Clumsily to begin with, the monster passed barely off

the ground over Apt now emptied of people. It went on up the valley, avoiding the mountain of Lure where – no doubt to its knowledge – there lived another dragon-hunting monk, Saint Donat, and turned above Sisteron. And the blood from its many wounds fell like rain upon Forcalquier; and the sound of its wings beating slowly and arhythmically shook the bastion walls of fortress towns, and their shadow brought moles from their holes with the thought that it was night. And in the end the monster disappeared out of the skies above Provence, in the direction of the high Alpine peaks where it thought to hide itself away.

But it had presumed too much upon its own strength, and altitude and intense cold did nothing for the huge creature as its powers began to fail it. Rendered sightless by pain, it dropped out of the sky like a thunderbolt, and the gigantic body, its joints all dislocated, crashed down on to a tiny village whose inhabitants thought the end of the world was upon them.

This place was the highest in Europe, the spire of its bell-tower being more than two hundred metres above sea-level, and it was so wretched, so far removed from the world, so little known that it did not even possess a name. But when the corpse of the Giant Worm had finally rotted away, after many months in which the fresh air of those altitudes had driven away the fetid stench, and when the mountain folk – who were so attached to their native place – had rebuilt their chalets, the village was given the name of Saint Véran, in honour of the Bishop.

ITALIAN CAPRICE
Part Two

INTO ITALY

And so, eventually, with the long haul across France behind them, and all the episodes and experiences of that rich time now reduced to memories, they turned eastwards, towards Italy.

And, considering again the matter of degrees of difference, of climate, geography, manners and civilisation, Julian Greenwood contemplated the even more dramatic transition from the French ways to which, over the months of their stay there, his charges had so amiably accommodated themselves, to the spectacular, multi-coloured world of gorgeous, overwhelming historicity into which their travels would now plunge them.

For Italy, quite rightly, was the focus of the Tour as Julian had himself experienced it, and as he had planned this one.

There, beyond the mountains which bracketed the northern reaches, across the sea which, he had finally decided, would afford them access via Liguria, lay a land of fabulous content - the ambiguity of that being quite deliberate– in which the origins and evolution of their European civilisation were made manifest in every conceivable aspect, from ancient time through the medieval and Renaissance right up to now, *Anno Domini* 1786.

There was, of course, infinitely too much to comprehend in the months available to them. They were to be domiciled in Florence to begin with, in lodgings as central as Julian had been able to contrive. There would be time and opportunity for excursions away from that base, to Sienna for the Palio, perhaps, that thundering riot of a horserace around the piazza in July; to San Gimignano for its medieval alleyways and fortified towers and the appalling, unspeakable frescoes in the cathedral there, depicting the tortures of the damned in Hell, and the lovely, incomparable views of the vineyards of Chianti below the town; to various Etruscan sites such as Volterra and others which, Julian knew, would appeal to the antiquary in Sebastian. And then there would be the proud city of Florence itself.

Julian realised, with some urgency now, that a planned, coherent viewing of that city and its inestimable treasures would be essential if the young men were not simply to stand nonplussed and amazed by a dream wealth of significances completely closed off to them for their lack of knowledge. How frequently must the Grand Tour of Foreign Parts have amounted effectively to nothing more than a prolonged, youthful male jollification against a backdrop of incomparable riches – artistic, architectural, historical, literary – ignored for want of informed interest, or treated to merely the most cavalier, casual glance *en passant* in the hectic dash to rendezvous with friends from home and drink the day away in the reassurance of their English company. But that was simply not the way to foster or encourage the kind of adult independence which Julian had in mind for his young men, who fortunately anyway did not seem unduly that way inclined. And here he acknowledged that their success in achieving, both of them, a hugely improved mastery of the French language had imparted confidence and self-esteem. Julian was particularly gratified where Edward was concerned, and he gave thanks to such powers as may be for the boy's susceptibility to the charms of young women. The occasional outings into the arms of professional practitioners of the arts of *Eros* were as nothing when measured against the positive gains in the matter of language.

Charles de Ménars had not been remiss in advising Julian of the likelihood of such escapades, having rightly assumed that his own sons, the irrepressible Philippe and Aurélien, would have happily imparted intelligence of such possibilities.

*

I find it hard to believe, wrote Sebastian, *that France is effectively at an end for us, and that we now enter into an experience, of Italy, which is like to prove even more opulent, if that is possible, in what it has to offer than this first, French phase has been. In the months we have spent away we have lived, it seems to me, more than a life-time's worth of novel experience, adventure and enjoyment. For indeed the French cousins – both Ned's and ours – the splendid residences which have been as home to us, have become, for myself certainly, an integral part of the furniture of private memory.*

I know that this is true of Ned also, even if the emphases in his patterns of recollection do differ from mine. So, what impressions particularly must needs be set down in this close retrospect before they fade, for all their pleasurable intensity, as they inevitably will? The novelty of living a French life for the first time, in Paris; the exquisite kindness and polish of the Châtigny family – the pleasure of keeping company with Gautier, the confirmed brilliance of Maître Courtois, the genteel, ladylike sweetness of Mademoiselle Clothilde – and what a consort she could make for dear old Nedward – except that Lord Withybrook would never allow him a union with a Papist! Then our own cousins, and 'mon Loyre gaulois' indeed! Only now do I comprehend my Uncle Greenwood's observations on M. du Bellay's sonnet, for the Loire does become a feature in the personal landscape of memory, with Philippe and Aurélien, Jeanne and Chantal and their much loved, bizarre old games, and the thrill of an early point across country, a glorious, exhilarating gallop with the prospect of a kill at the end of it, and the meat apportioned by Uncle Charles to the tenants and hunt servants. How I should have loved to stay for the wine-harvest in the autumn to come. But it is in the nature of this undertaking that one moves on, inevitably too soon, it seems. I shall return, though, in later years, and hunt again at Ménars, and see Count Charles and his English lady grown old, and Philippe and Aurélien married and established, and the little girls become fine ladies, with noble husbands and children.

And then, not least, the spectacular transition from the Loire to Provence, the exquisite hotel close by the Place d'Albertas, and, of course, the house of Madame X... with lovely, lovable Sylvie, so willing and so adept at her delicious art, so sunnily good-humoured, such a delight to be with. Truly, the climate of the Midi does make for an enhancement of ones appreciation of the flesh and all that goes with it. But it is as well, probably, not to pay the same visit too frequently; one of the more puzzling paradoxes of life, that.

In ideal circumstances: 'Had we but world enough, and Time...' there would now be a long interlude before we moved on into Italy, which is after all the goal and focus of our undertaking. And this preliminary smack of Provence with its Roman dimension does afford some intimation of the likely impression Italy must surely make upon travellers who, although from more northerly regions, will usually be steeped, positively steeped in the civilisation, lore and languages of the ancient world of the Mediterranean. Latin has, of course, long been an essential part of the machinery of government in the post-Renaissance world of northern Europe - hence the 'grammar' schools, those hugely effective instruments of practical instruction. But if one looks beyond all that, to the living, spoken language that Latin once was - and how could one read Juvenal intelligently –or Catullus! – any *other way? One cannot but discern something of the brilliant, sun-bathed, colourful vitality of the world of 'Rome'. And indeed, knowing more than a little something of that world already, I am apprehensive of Italy and all it will have to reveal to me. The thought of standing among the ruins of the Colosseum, for instance, will, I know, when the time comes, fill me with dread, for it will surely be - how could it not? - as if oneself were about to be offered up for mutilation and hideous death, and all for the unspeakable delectation of the vile, vile mob. The amphitheatres at Nimes and Arles were indication enough that this will be so; that sense of thousands of spectators avid for blood, pain and horror, revelling in the desperation and agony of human quarry is something which one senses as very real there. And indeed, the spectacle of such degradation so eagerly entered into must have left many of the victims only too happy to bid this world farewell. The hunting beasts loosed into the arena were at least blameless by comparison with the human ghouls who gorged upon the sight of their slaughter. Yet, for all that, the Roman legacy, the contribution of Rome to our own contemporary world has been immense...*

Paradox and complexity indeed! One cannot but fall back upon the sanity and rationality of the Greeks, and yet again, there, too... Some days ago we reconnoitred the border at Menton, or Mentone, as it also known. My lasting impression is likely to be of the brilliantly coloured houses which give on to the waterfront – green shutters with rich ochre and terracotta facades, colours which positively vibrate in the intense sunlight of the Mediterranean. And already, one felt, they spoke to us of a style of perception, and with that a moral attitude, very different even from Provence, without mentioning the rest of France so laboriously traversed. For much of France, I now realise, is simply not good at colour, not by comparison with what seems to be store in the Italian phase

105

anyway; of course the natural colours of the landscape are as one finds them, and frequently magnificent they are too, but the man-made things do speak to us of man, and one recalls all that northern grey stone, and the inevitable brown paint.

Clearly though, Italians see things quite differently – it is hardly surprising that theirs is the civilisation from which so much in the way of superlative painting derives, one saw it and understood it in that instant, with the briefest glimpse of those facades. And thus, in a matter of yards, the distinctive character of the novel ambiance, or ambienza, *as I must now learn to say! - of Italy had asserted itself. The background of mountain, sea and sky was really not so different, but what the architecture conveyed was a very particular notion of an identity that was decidedly not French. This was something of a shock; we have become so accustomed, over the months, to what has impressed itself upon our minds as familiar and even homely – for we have become sufficiently cosmopolitan to acknowledge that 'home' can be found in other places than home in the sense, for us, of Lancashire, Warwickshire, or Hertfordshire. And I recall with pleasure that delicious French phrase, 'à la maison'. 'On rentre à la maison'. 'Ce soir on dîne à la maison.' And now we face another dramatic shift in our perception of the immediate world around us. We have made a more than passable effort, I would say, in our time away from England, at adapting to French ways – even to learning how to eat with cutlery laid the wrong way up to display the family coat of arms! Now, with the fabulous incentive of Italy before us, we are to make that effort again, to substitute entirely novel assumptions for those others acquired here...*

VIGNETTE
Florence

In a post house in the hills above Florence Julian Greenwood gave his young men their first detailed briefing on that city, so miraculous a monument to the Renaissance of the fifteenth century, with its writers, artists, sculptors and thinkers, its bankers and merchants.

"In the time we spend in Florence," he began, "we shall acquire, day by day, a sense of what the city is about in terms of its artistic and historical significance. But in order to be able to do this we must first identify a number of considerations - not too many, but enough to contrive a coherent and sensible *entrée* into a proper understanding of the things of this place. So, the cathedral for instance, with its dome by Brunelleschi not unknown to Sir Christopher Wren, by the way, if you care to pursue that one; the Piazza della Signoria and Palazzo Vecchio, the political centre. Florence in its heyday was, of course, a republic; it has no aristocracy, being ruled by its citizens, but it was effectively an oligarchy, a state ruled by its wealthiest subjects – as usually tends to be the case. Venice, by contrast, does have what is to all intents and purposes an aristocracy, or at least, a patrician caste – of families named in the Golden Book, the *libro d'oro,* from which its leaders both political and military are chosen. You could not command a Venetian war-galley, gentlemen, unless your name featured in those pages. Shakespeare's Othello, the Moor of Venice was, you will appreciate, exceptional, being a mercenary general of armies; the Venetians were wise enough to know when the rules might be put aside to accommodate superlative expertise in the interests of the state. But, to return to Florence, the city and state were ruled by a dynasty, the banking family of Medici, from the time of Cosimo in the late fourteenth century until a mere fifty years ago, or so.

So, an elite may not necessarily call itself an aristocracy, or bedeck itself with those labels of rank and title which do tend to be typical of such a caste, but it is still an elite – of the best people as they perceive themselves to be – the *aristoi* in the original Greek, even if a man's proudest boast is to call himself 'citizen'. The artists, of course, were perceived as artisans, and were decidedly not of the great. Savants and scholars were somewhat more highly regarded, and often even participated in government, as did Machiavelli, of whom more shortly. However, the history of this city is of an exceptional kind, almost indeed exceptional enough to justify the Florentines' extraordinarily high opinion of themselves, and I would have you take it in and make it a part of your private and personal equipment, if I may so express myself. Where you are concerned, Edward, I would draw your attention first to one Baldassare Castiglione, the cavalry officer, remember, who deliberated upon the perfect virtues of the civilised man, and then Machiavelli, Niccolò Machiavelli, a high functionary of government, who wrote about politics and how men conduct themselves in the pursuit of power. And, sir, about war. Machiavelli on war is not to be despised, gentlemen, and there may be much there to reward you for any effort you may care to make in that direction.

For you, Sebastian, we might perhaps endeavour to make a start with Leon Battista Alberti on painting, *Della Pittura.* No doubt Horace Mann will be able to advise on English translations of these texts, and we might attempt a dual approach, don't you think, if we lay the English side by side with the Italian? And in that way, sir, you will acquire the language as you take in the content of the master's deliberations."

"Horace Mann, sir?"

"Sir Horace Mann, Edward. The English Resident. A man

of distinction, consequence and much cultivation, an old friend, in fact, who is well known for the help he has always been in the habit of so willingly affording to English travellers such as ourselves. And if you were thinking, sir, that all of this is somewhat removed from the style of life which is more usually associated with the young officer, or officer to be, you may care to consider that the further up the military hierarchy you proceed, the more useful you will find any knowledge of the languages of Europe you care to acquire - and I am happy to be able to remark upon the signal success of your efforts with the French - not to mention any acquaintance and familiarity you may gain with a world somewhat more cosmopolitan and of decidedly greater fascination than that of the bone-headed cadet who spends his off-duty hours betting, ratting, drinking and whoring, tossing for shillings with a bull-dog pup at his heels. Not that I have anything against bull-dog pups, I hasten to add, nor against a wager, either. But you shall be more than cannon-fodder, sir, which is precisely what such young gentlemen are - no more, no less - in the eyes of canny commanders. And besides, that great world is where advancement is to be found, and honour to redound to your name."

"I never imagined I should pass for a scholar, sir."

"One may cultivate the interests I have described, Edward, without fear, I think, of such ignominy."

But here Edward, battling with his bemusement at the unaccustomed praise so deftly and lightly bestowed upon him, and with his dismay at the thought of the spectre of the black-clad scribbler hovering so eagerly over him, completely missed Julian's irony.

"...And then again, sir, one day you will succeed to your father's title. Do you wish to spend your days as some species of aristocratic Squire Western, of Mr Fielding's novel? Or would you prefer to bring lustre to your name, sir, by moving in the most brilliant circles which could be open to you, not merely by dint of birth, since the Withybrook earldom, if I may put it thus, is not all that venerable, but by virtue of the sound years of military service which will have been yours, plus your knowledge of the world, your acquaintance with at least two of Europe's great languages, and the cosmopolitan polish of your manners?"

"With Castiglione behind you you can hardly fail, you know, Farrell!"

"Sebastian!" The anger in Mr Greenwood's rebuke was unmistakeable; Sebastian was chastened.

"I do beg your pardon, sir. That was quite uncalled for, and I blush for it. But, if I may say so, what a vision of the future you hold out there!"

"Mr Greenwood, you will allow me to say that I have never been spoken to in that manner before, and I am quite overwhelmed by your words."

"My dear boy, I do assure you that my intention in speaking thus is of the very best. I press you, I know, but only because I have come to consider you capable, sir, of living up to what I would wish you to envisage in a perspective of the future which has perhaps not occurred to you prior to this. Had I not believed you equal to the challenge this represents, I should not have spoken out - for it would have been cruel indeed to raise hopes where none were due - and we could have continued upon our way in amiable, amicable inconsequential. As it is I pay you my best compliment, sir. Truly."

Julian smiled down at the young man before him – Ned, with his bulging blue eyes and never quite tidy head of hair – willing him to come to terms with the truth of what had just been voiced.

"*You* compliment *me,* sir?"

The incredulity behind the question caught at Julian's throat. He looked straight at Edward.

"I do, sir," he said.

There was a moment's silence, memorable for the shared warmth of it, then Julian went on, "So, gentlemen, moving on then, from the Palazzo Vecchio, the Old Palace, if you wish, but the seat of government anyway - and I shall say no more of this until you have set eyes on it, for reasons that will become apparent– we come to the river of Florence, the Arno, to cross by the Ponte Vecchio and make for the Pitti Palace and Boboli Gardens beyond. And that, gentlemen, must afford us the essentials of a plan of orientation. We shall pay our respects to Sir Horace Mann, of course, and he will no doubt be delighted to discuss these matters with us. Our object will not be to hasten perfunctorily round everything there is to be seen in Florence -a proper appreciation of this city and its treasures would require a residence of very considerably longer than we have available to us- but to see what will leave a lasting impression of the most important things. Then, who knows? One day you may choose to return, in order to delve more deeply into the art, architecture, literature and history of what is after allone of the truly great cities of the world. Or quite simply to enjoy it. For it is, as you shall see, quite exquisitely splendid. And you, Sebastian, assuming your interest develops as it well may, could decide in due course to return and reside here for such a longer period; there are noteworthy precedents, sir, and there are not all that many places in this world where one could be more content than in a Florentine villa.

"I shall give it the most serious consideration, sir."

"Come and visit you, man. On leave, one day."

"Nothing would please me more, Nedward. We shall laze away our days, in some exquisite villa, in a garden with statues... and grottoes, and a moss-grown lion-fountain belching forth crystal streams..."

"No, no, Sebastian! That's the door-knocker!"

"What? Belching forth... et cetera?"

"No, man. Of course..." Edward caught sight of Mr Greenwood and Sebastian grinning at him, and stopped abruptly.

"Damme, sir! You should go for the Bar, by God! You have all the tricks of the shyster to you."

"Thank you, Ned. I had considered it, I will allow. But I shall most likely devote myself to a studious private independence, I think. Independence being the principal consideration there. And I may well live a while abroad, if I choose to."

"Choice is all, is it not?" asked Mr Greenwood. "You see before you, Edward, a most fortunate gentleman. You and I, sir, are constrained by an inheritance, you by a title and a great estate, I by a more modest though not insubstantial manor where I oversee the tenancies of several farms and administer justice as my position requires me to do. The key to content, if I may put it thus, is to make the most of ones circumstances, whatsoever they may be. Sebastian's independence has its undoubted advantages, and very considerable they are, but you and I, sir, may be happy in our respective stations. You have it in you, Edward, to make a fine soldier, and perhaps even eventually, circumstances permitting, a commander. Therefore it is meet you should relish the prospect."

"I long for it, sir."

"And so you should, my dear boy. So you should."

*

Dear Miss Westlake, the letter began, *I trust you will forgive me for the liberty I take in approaching you thus when I make it clear that I do so in the interest of our mutual friend, Mrs Harriet de Savigny.*

During the course of recent travels away from my home here in Torri del Benaco, I had cause to find myself briefly in the proximity of an Englishman of decidedly equivocal aspect, a gentleman, I must reluctantly allow, even if the intemperate nature of his conduct could not but bring the most regrettable discredit upon that station.

Madam, I should not be writing this letter now, had it not been made known to me that this was Peter de Savigny, a dispossessed English 'milord' who at that very moment was loudly expressing his intentions of ingratiating himself with his ageing father by seeking out a wayward wife, who had most shamefully abandoned him, and fathering a male child on her, willy-nilly.

I will allow, Madam, that my first thought upon being apprised of these things was to contrive a clash of some kind between us, and take appropriate and decisive action against him. I then realised, however - and I am sure you will appreciate and understand my reasons for this - that I could hardly do so then and there without quite possibly compromising Mrs de Savigny in a way too obvious to be contemplated. Be assured though, Madam, that this is not to imply that I have done with Savigny. I do not deign to hunt him, but I shall be 'aux aguets', on the watch for him, and next time he shall not escape me.

Now clearly, I may not write to the lady; it was agreed between us some considerable time ago now that there should be no further communication between us, although I did offer her such protection as I may properly afford to her in her abandoned state. She, in her independence, made it known to me that she would not avail herself of this, and we parted on that understanding. I write to you therefore - as one described to me with great affection as an old and trusted friend – in the hope that you will see fit to apprise her of her husband's intent.

Perhaps, Madam, I may hope that you will honour me with the favour of a reply to this missive?

I am, Madam, yours most respectfully,
Fabrizio di Benaco

Isabella Westlake reclined in her usual chaise on the balcony of her villa high above village and sea and pondered this development. There was, it seemed, a threat abroad and stalking Harriet - not that Peter de Savigny had not probably given voice to similar intentions previously, under the influence of wine, or whatever else it was he chose to seek his personal oblivion through. Isabella was in no doubt as to what particular kind of insane ravings Prince Fabrizio had been witness to. Briefly she wondered what kind of milieu it could have been that had found two such disparate men in close company, then she put the thought from her mind, in the knowledge that there did exist exploits of a kind to entice gentlemen in search of self-indulgence to which ladies were simply not party.

Prince Fabrizio, tactfully, had made no mention of a specific *locale* but, obliquely as he phrased his intention vis-à-vis Savigny, he had left Isabella in no doubt as to what that was. And she knew without question that his outrage and contempt for a man, who by reputation throughout Europe repeatedly traduced in the most blatant fashion the standards of behaviour and the values of a proud caste, would combine with his continued concern for one he had loved to lead him to provoke a duel in which he might kill her friend's renegade spouse. Behind the matter-of-fact words of the Prince's careful phrasings Isabella sensed the implacable purpose inherited from an ancient lineage of warrior aristocracy, sensed also the tender concern and quality of feeling he still entertained for Harriet who, she understood, had been his partner in love of a kind she herself had never experienced. For, she now recollected, there had been something transfigured about Harriet at the time of her liaison with Fabrizio. Oh, to have been loved in that way! To have experienced what her dear friend had contrived only to hint at, albeit in such a way as to leave her *confidante* in no doubt as to the marvel of it. And that, too, Isabella understood, had been a simple matter of fact, as matter of fact as Fabrizio's intention of killing Peter de Savigny to ensure Harriet should come to no harm from him. In the balmy April warmth of her Mediterranean retreat, Isabella Westlake shuddered at the thought of what the Prince's letter had brought with it.

She would write to Harriet, currently with her cousins in the Loire Valley, and urge her to make haste in her progress southwards. And, much as she genuinely deplored the circumstances which had prompted Prince Fabrizio to take so uncompromising a step in writing to her in that vein, Isabella, with that wry sense of irony engendered by her own condition, understood that the opportunity now afforded her to initiate some measure of forewarning for her dear friend - so that she, too might be *aux aguets* – did in some small but not insignificant way bring her back into the action of life, render her not entirely superfluous. And there, that morning, in her exquisite, flower bedecked, dazzlingly multi-coloured bower of despond, her spirits rose.

She did of course recall the Honourable Peter de Savigny from the time when, as an improbably handsome cornet of Blues, he had paid court to the brilliant Miss Haverhill. She herself had been in those days a sought-after member of fashionable London circles, the more so than Harriet in fact, given her enormous wealth, from the time when the two of them together had finally quitted their 'Academy For Young Ladies' to take their place in the world. And she recalled how everyone had envied her friend the god-like young man who had so assiduously paid court to her. They had met, Harriet and Peter, at brilliant *soirées* of one kind or another in the great houses of London society to which Isabella had introduced Harriet, and had rapidly become the focus of envious attention amongst the 'ton'. But even so, Isabella now recalled, there had been those whose perception of Savigny had not been without reservations; he was observed, by those in the know about these things, to frequent guardee circles which were not of the most stable kind. And there had been rumours of huge debauches, gaming for enormous stakes, unsavoury connections of various kinds. But the magnetism of the couple's beauty, the lubricious excitement their attraction had prompted, had carried them into a splendid match, the wedding of the moment, an exquisite town house gifted by Lord Hawkhurst – avid for an heir - within easy reach of the Park.

And duly, Charlotte was born – not the boy for whom the elderly Hawkhursts longed, but nevertheless... And of course there would be further children.

But there were not. And as Isabella's deadly ailment tightened its grip on her, so Peter and Harriet had moved rapidly apart. She, Isabella, had withdrawn from English social life, taken up residence at the lovely Villa des Pins perched high above the sea at Roquebrune, a retreat of such timeless splendour that, in her better moments she could almost be grateful for the necessity which had confined her there.

And Harriet, dearest Harriet had been a mainstay of unremitting love and affection in her loneliness. Out of the timorous bond of mutual liking which had brought two frightened, lonely little girls together in the school years of their early adolescence there had grown a love of such strength as would most likely endure to Isabella's probable premature death. As she sat in her sweet Mediterranean sunshine and pondered these things, Isabella began to understand something of what her death might mean to Harriet - whose exploits and adventures since her estrangement from Peter had surely been indication enough already of a certain discontent, had she only had the acuityto see what had been patently obvious. And she was ashamed at the self-absorption which had caused her to ignore her friend's need. But at least her Christmas gift of money had enabled her dearest Harriet to extricate herself from the kind of embarrassment over gaming debts that would otherwise have had her in its degrading trap. That had been a genuine act of affection, Isabella knew, even if the sum in question had been as nothing to her. Now she longed for the sound of the carriage arriving, the servant's announcement, *"Madame de Savigny, Madame"*, the sight of Harriet sweeping into the house and into her arms... the tears, the laughter, warmth, love... It had been hardly surprising that Fabrizio di Benaco had made Harriet the object of his affections, or that she had responded as she had. For it was the strength of her, as Isabella perceived it, despite the disappointment of her marriage and the ensuing discontent and unhappiness, the strength of her, the undaunted will-power, that one remembered. And Harriet deserved better of life than she had so far had. Of that there was no question.

And as she penned her letter to her friend at Ménars, Isabella felt herself possessed by the happiness of Spring, with its promise of a new start to things.

*

In the warm, sunlit grounds of the Chateau de Ménars, at the 'ancient games place', the '*coin des jeux du temps jadis*', to which she had as usual been cajoled by the little girls, Jeanne and Chantal, Harriet read Isabella's letter and found herself not a little agitated by its content. But, much as there was to be weighed and considered there, she found herself quite incapable in the first instance of doing anything more than remaining seated, perfectly composed to all appearances, and watching her young French cousins as they played the knobbly ball game, the *jeu du boulet à boules.*

They were experimenting, she realised, with a variety of styles of delivery, drawing upon recollections of attempts by Sebastian and Edward to develop techniques for coping with the unpredictable bounce of the knobbly ball as it pitched on to the uneven surface of the table.

There were, it seemed, a number of options. You could go for a full toss, as in cricket, in the hope of a hole-in-one – but here one might be forgiven, Harriet thought, for the view that this was somewhat in the way of a desperate ploy, since the likelihood of a successful 'drop' was minimal. Although one did have to allow that the scatter technique of a drop from on high into a cluster of adversary bowls around the jack was a common practice in *boules,* that it did have, also, the advantage of cutting out of consideration the uneven surface of the table as well as the random behaviour of the knobbly ball, the *boulet,* itself.

There were other possibilities: you could pitch for the central hole with one bounce and no more, in the hope that such minimal randomness might favour you, although Harriet had never actually witnessed such an event; or, you could dribble the exasperating *boulet* with a calculated minimum forward movement up to the target hole, in the hope that it may topple tiredly in; or align the *boulet* in such a way as possibly to minimise the irregular effect of the knobbly bounce, and roll the object briskly down the centre of the table in the hope of taking advantage of the trough-like configuration of its uneven surface.

From the little girls' conversation now overheard by Harriet, it appeared that Edward had worked out these various possibilities, to the incredulous amazement of the Ménars sons, who it seemed had found it quite beyond comprehension that the Englishmen should apply themselves so purposefully and with such obvious enjoyment to matters of such trivial moment. Harriet marvelled; the young man must have explained it in French, otherwise the little girls could never have grasped the implications of each option so comprehensively. Could this *Edouard* have been the tiresome young rakehell and pugilist Lord Withybrook had complained of, when he had bribed her to foist him upon Julian and Sebastian? Clearly, the little girls had adored the *milords,* as they persisted in calling them.

"*Non! C'est comme ça qu'il a fait, Edouard!*"

"*Bon, alors! Si on y réssuit, on le nomme 'la botte d'Edouard'!*"

"*Et on le lui dira.*" "*Mais bien sûr!*"

And there at least, then, was something she had got supremely right. And it was not, she decided now, that she was afraid of Peter who, the last time they had spent together had shown himself only too capable of the kind of semi-demented, ineffectual raving described in Isabella's letter.

What did give her real cause for fear was Fabrizio. Because Harriet knew, as a matter of certainty, that if he, Fabrizio, took it into his head to kill Peter then he would surely do so. For in Fabrizio, she now recalled, there had always been a deliciously undeviating sense of purpose about the way he led his life both in terms of pleasure and obligation. And Peter's death simply must not occur too soon. He must be alive, at least, somewhere, at the time she, Harriet planned to entice her stallion, Sebastian, into her bed once more. So, could one rely on circumstance, in all its giddy unpredictability, to keep Peter and Fabrizio apart over the next nine months or so, at least until Harriet was able to effect her purpose with Sebastian wherever she might contrive it? It had after all been improbably unfortunate that Fabrizio should have been witness to such an exhibition as Peter was capable of. For truly there was, she was convinced, an element of dementia there, something from which people had been known to shy away in horror and contempt; the spectacle of a once god-like young man now degraded almost to the point of lunacy by the remorseless demon within him which had turned him away from the abundance of every kind of riches and worldly consequence which his birth had put in his way. Harriet recalled the wonderful portrait of Peter at Hawkhurst Savigny, as it had been before the old earl had caused it to be removed and consigned to the oblivion of a cellar beneath the great house, Adonis himself by Pompeo Batoni, attired in the uniform of a cornet of Blues. Could she possibly leave things entirely to chance, when what was in question was crucial to her own future happiness and well-being? And that of Charlotte?

The matter did require further deliberation, but Harriet had never been one to leave things to take their own course. So, her first act must be to ascertain the whereabouts of the travelling party at the moment. And if she could engineer a *rencontre* sooner than Venice, there was no reason why she should not make use of Sebastian in the way she had already planned. An earlier encounter would after all forestall any attempt that Fabrizio might be inclined to make on the life of Peter. Only, what a pity, when all was said and done, that he, Fabrizio could not have been the one to impregnate her; and she recalled the delirious embraces of their lovers' summer at Torri del Benaco with an exquisite *frisson* of arousal and regret. But Sebastian would serve her purpose; there would be nothing in so momentary a union of the wonder and mystery which Fabrizio's age-old knowingness had brought to that summer, when she, Harriet, had been made to realise the sheer inadequacy of what Peter had had to offer even from their first moments together as man and wife. But Sebastian, an ingenuous but enthusiastic practitioner, would take what she had to offer and enter her, she thought, with no more compunction or ulterior motive than he would feel in playing an innings at cricket, or engaging in a bout at the foils with Edward Farrell. Harriet allowed herself a brief moment of private amusement as she recalled their joint efforts to free a truly stupendous erection from a rather tight pair of breeches. And the size of it, when it had eventually swung free!... She gave a naughty giggle of delight at the memory. No wonder the *lingam* was an object of worship and reverence in the Hindu culture of the Indies. Fabrizio had explained that, and other aspects of oriental erotic lore to her in a manner which, implicitly she had understood, simply dismissed the Catholic obsession with sexual guilt as of no relevance whatsoever to what she, Harriet, knew to be the true facts of the matter as properly celebrated in 'heathen' belief.

One might well have expected Fabrizio, as a native aristocrat, to have taken rather a different line, but he had been possessed of both the intellect and the imagination to take him out into the world at large and bring him into contact with other styles of perception which in their time were just beginning to impinge upon what had been hitherto an implacably self-regarding European awareness, as gentlemen explorers such as Louis-Antoine de Bougainville and Théophile de Granville had begun to strike out beyond the limits – both geographical and otherwise – of the old world. And it did remain self-evidently the case that, in love-making between man and woman, in the physical acts involved in the preliminary caresses of affection which led to the moment of penetration, and in the subsequent intensification of mutual passion as it mounted to the climax of orgasm, there existed ways – appreciatively and enthusiastically documented and evaluated in oriental texts by and large reviled and demonised in a Church-dominated Europe - of ensuring degrees of reciprocal pleasure to heighten the erotic quality of any union. This was part of the scheme of things, God's scheme, if you wished. Fabrizio had understood all this, and had instructed Harriet accordingly. Peter had known nothing of any of it, nor would he have wished to. Adonis to all appearances, but Peter de Savigny had been no Greek. The facts of matter remained nevertheless incontrovertible. 'So, let us then to bodies go...' Doctor Donne, the great erotic poet of the previous century, as so frequently and exceptionally, had the truth of it.

Charles de Ménars, she thought, would most probably be able to give her some idea of the present whereabouts of Julian and his charges, even if only approximately. Poor, dear Isabella should be kept right out of things for the moment. Should her plans result in the desired end, a son and heir to the Hawkhurst title and estates, Isabella should be gently apprised of the means by which the business had been effected, assuming of course that she would still be alive and sufficiently *au fait* with the world for it to matter. Certainly Isabella had been horrified and appalled by what Fabrizio had seen fit to impart to her; she would shed no tears for Peter de Savigny. But the details and technicalities were not for invalid ladies of delicate nurture. And with this thought Harriet understood just how much her own situation as an abandoned wife had constrained her into a life of survival lived off the wits, and off such opportunities and adventures as one felt bold enough to engage with. Not that there had not always been something of that about her, Harriet knew, by contrast with her beloved friend. For the spoof memoirs of certain ladies of opportunity penned by inventive men of broad sympathies earlier in the century had delighted her from an early age when, advised and guided by older girls at the Academy who had taken a close emotional interest in her handsome young self, she had first browsed with lubricious excitement through the pages of forbidden texts. Clearly, these had struck some chord of familiarity deep within her; now, she understood, the words of those texts had gone to the very heart of her identity, of her own sense of who and what she was, she, Harriet de Savigny, nee Haverhill. Roxana, Moll Flanders, Fanny Hill, even Clarissa Harlowe and Pamela, they all, whatever their station and circumstances, were one way or another facets of her own most private person. Harriet paused briefly to marvel, like the connoisseur she was, at the genius of that motley collection of individuals who had brought them into being. Then, lighter of heart now, she left the little girls to their knobbly ball game – still apparently proceeding with unremitting *élan* - and went in search of her cousin, Charles de Ménars.

ROME

From Florence the Greenwood party was in process, in leisurely style, of making its way southwards to Rome, where they were to spend several months. Meanwhile they would sojourn briefly in Sienna, make excursions out from there to such places as San Gimignano and Volterra, learn what they could of the Etruscans and move on via Orvieto and further places of interest and curiosity into Lazio itself.

Florence had been more than a little overwhelming, Julian had to allow, by virtue of the sheer volume of what it had to offer and the consequent amount of knowledge it would have proved necessary to possess oneself of, if one had aimed to make complete sense of the brilliant treasures of art and architecture on which the city so rightly prided itself. Had they been foolhardy enough to adopt such an approach the effort required to encompass such a quantity of information would quickly have turned the Tour into something quite other than what had always been intended. Julian was a firm believer, he discovered, in the efficacy of pleasurable experience. At Westminster the boys would presumably have had their Latin beaten into them; this was in no way intended as an extension of those years, however eager one may be to have them understand and appreciate.

So, once again Julian found himself pondering an overwhelming question, the question, this time, of Rome, and where to begin. There were those of his acquaintance, he knew, who had simply shipped off their sons and friends with a hired tutor and left them to get on with it. And how many participants in the Tour had allowed themselves, in following the fashion in so uninformed a way, to lay out huge sums in expenditure on travel of a kind which could be of no conceivable value? Young English *milordi* were perfectly capable of getting drunk, losing at the gaming tables and picking up the pox without leaving their native shores. The notion of the Grand Tour of Foreign Parts was in itself an admirable one, of that Julian was in no doubt. That there were different ways of going about it was equally obvious, and whilst he had no intention of allowing Sebastian and Edward excessive freedoms, he certainly did not wish to dragoon them into any commitment of a kind to leave only a sullen resentment and a spoiled recollection of what he hoped would remain a lifelong memory of happy times for them. The experiences of the Tour properly conducted could provide Sebastian with something of the guidance he might need to enable him to lead an independent life of scholarship and philosophy; equally, they could contribute to the making, in Edward, of a more effective and finer soldier than he might, without it, have had it in him to become. For, beneath the glitter and spectacle of fashionable aristocratic life in England there were too many of the 'milords' who amounted to very little, so constrained were they in their thinking by convention and precedent slavishly adhered to. And Julian recollected Edward's words all those long months ago at the Bell in Bromley, when he had spoken of his father's pronouncements on wine.

"My father, sir, drinks only French wine. He would maintain that such others as exist are simply not for gentlemen." What a long way Edward had travelled, in more senses than one, since that moment. And indeed, both boys had done prodigiously well; Sebastian, linguist and classical scholar, had already made substantial inroads into the task of acquiring the Italian language; Edward, amazed at his newly acquired facility in French, worked manfully at his Latin, now read the less complex authors with some degree of confidence and was beginning to show real interest in the military writers. For him, Julian understood, the French phase of the Tour would most likely remain the highlight of their two years away, given the affectionate relations he had established with both sets of cousins – and here Julian wryly recalled his own heart-stopping apprehensions as he had watched Edward instruct both Philippe and Aurélien de Ménars in the noble English art of fisticuffs – and given also the ease with which he had found he could acquire their language, French, which at school had left him flummoxed and humiliated.

And then, most pleasing of all, there was the genuine self-assurance born of decent consideration and treatment which had replaced the braggart self-assertion of one whose life thus far had by no means been all it might have been, despite the rank which he was now learning to bear with real dignity and grace. Previously Withybrook might have bought the boy into the Horse Guards willy-nilly, since that was the way of the Army; now the Horse Guards would be fortunate indeed to acquire such a young man. And Lord Withybrook might well marvel, at such time as he received his son back. Although probably he would not.

The susceptibilities of that noble earl were not a matter of any consequence to Julian Greenwood; the future of Edward Farrell, he acknowledged, was. And he understood, with perhaps just a *soupçon* of regret, that such might have been his own son, had he chosen to marry.

He reverted to the question which had been preoccupying him, the question as to how he might best approach the matter of Rome with his young men. Their classical studies at Westminster would have provided them with much in the way of a rudimentary body of knowledge that might be assumed. For, the notion of 'Rome' to an Englishman of some degree of cultivation must be as familiar, Julian mused, as anything in his sense of his own history. The notion of a spiritual empire of the Church modelled on the secular empire of antiquity which had inspired the great builder-popes of the Renaissance to patronise the artists and architects who had created the magnificence so gawked at by the scions of the great dynasties of the north would be less so. There was, in England, a decided lack of inclination to treat anything pertaining to 'popery' with the open-minded curiosity and interest it might merit on other than religious grounds – historical, say, or aesthetic. Hardly surprising, he readily allowed, in view of the things which had transpired no more than two hundred years ago. And there had of course been a Greenwood forbear who had acted for Elizabeth's Walsingham. But then there was today. Go back not quite two hundred years, and you had Caravaggio, with his delicious renderings of low life in the Roman streets. Perhaps one might begin by warning the young men about beautiful, fortune-telling gypsy-girls, whose thieving grandmothers so adeptly picked your pocket from behind as you admired the young woman's grubby cleavage so enchantingly displayed before you? Julian chuckled as he thought of Edward. He made himself a fresh pipe of tobacco, put his feet up and continued his deliberations. Start in the present, then look at the past – both pasts, of antiquity and Renaissance – and ascertain how the distant past became today's present. This was the pattern of Edward Gibbon's book, as the author himself had explained it to Julian in London some years back. And that was, it appeared, in the way now of becoming something of a 'magnum opus'. And the old fellow was still at it, scribbling away in Lausanne.

"Another damned great thick book, I hear. Always scribble, scribble, scribble, eh, Mr Gibbon?"

Julian came close to choking upon his tobacco, as he recalled this comment from a Royal Duke, no less, on his old friend's literary endeavours. It was a pity that their route northwards and into the German-speaking lands would not take them by Lausanne.

However, the obvious thing, with Rome, was to make a start with the ancient Centre – Forum, Colosseum, Circus Maximus, Capitol. And with those would go the classical museums of the Palazzo Nuovo and the Palazzo dei

Conservatori . To acquire some familiarity with the geography of the centre would be to enter into a preliminary engagement with the history and meaning of the city through certain of its major landmarks. Sebastian, for instance, would be taken by the equestrian statue of the Emperor Marcus Aurelius on the Capitol Hill, and might well be led to read the Meditations of that philosophic ruler. In fact, Julian mused, knowing Sebastian as he now did, this was pretty well inevitable. And one might allow oneself to imagine that possibly an excursion in true Roman style to Tivoli on its hill-top once the summer heat had become overwhelming, and a saunter through the fabulous gardens of the Villa d'Este could well prompt Edward in later years perhaps to establish an Italian garden at Withybrook in the heart of Warwickshire. And so it should be again, as it had so frequently been in the past; for these were the ways in which the seeds of interest and admiration sown by the Tour took root in the minds of influential, wealthy young men and, germinating in the fullness of time, passed into the culture of their native lands far away.

From the balcony of their Sienna lodgings Julian looked over the crenellations of the city wall to a dazzling landscape punctuated with clusters of olive-trees in phalanx, with their gnarled, fantastical shapes, sturdy foot-soldiers of the local economy and, on the very hill-tops, outlined against a brilliant sky, the stately cypresses grouped, officer-like, above them. This was a landscape celebrated in a thousand paintings, a feature also, with Julian, of the template of private memory. For he too had had his Latin beaten into him at school; that had been as effective a part of the process by which he had come to be steeped in awareness of the ancient matrix of modern learning as any. There is nothing like terror, he mused wryly, to promote the habit of accurate recall of irregular verbs. And indeed the military wisdom absorbed from such writers as Caesar in Latin, Xenophon in Greek, could only have made itself available by dint of that preliminary, rote-learning labour. And now his young men were about it, and no doubt future generations would come to it in their turn. Julian was happy to be the agent of such continuity. He sat back in contentment and called for wine.

*

At the Villa des Pins Harriet de Savigny was writing a letter calculated to reach her cousin Julian Greenwood on his arrival in Rome.

Ostensibly her purpose in doing so was to inquire about the progress of the Tour so far; after all it was she who had urged it upon her recalcitrant brother back in Hertfordshire, she who had engineered the addition of Edward Farrell through her mediation with Lord and Lady Withybrook, acquaintances from the fashionable milieu from which now, thanks to the inestimable generosity and concern of Isabella, she had been able to free herself without obloquy. Her debt to her friend was, Harriet knew, incalculable; but at least it seemed that, since her arrival at Roquebrune, Isabella's spirits had taken a turn for the better, and Harriet knew, or hoped she knew, that the imminent prospect of her own presence in the house did account in no insignificant way for the modest dose of contentment which her friend now seemed to be enjoying.

In fact Harriet's purpose in writing to Julian was actually to ascertain the progress of the Tour and the likely chronology of its stages. If she could contrive a rendezvous with Sebastian somewhat earlier than next year's Carnival time at Venice that might be as well. With Peter on the loose and intent upon mischief and nuisance where she was concerned, that rendezvous did become all the more imperative, and most particularly in view of the fact that any further encounter between Fabrizio and Peter would most likely put an end to Harriet's plan. Quite simply, Peter must remain alive until Harriet had found the opportunity to mate with Sebastian. For preference, at all events. Harriet did still rather shy away from other possibilities, given her positive experiences with

Fabrizio and her negative ones with her husband.

Sebastian was at least a pleasant, acceptable young gentleman, no stranger to merriment and mischief, a most agreeable cavalier. And, eager as she was to please the elderly Hawkhursts, to secure the succession and be revenged upon Peter, she was not over eager to contrive this at any cost. Revenge, the Italians have it, is a dish best eaten cold, and there was absolutely no reason why the preparation should not be as exquisitely enjoyable as the eventual consumption of that particular feast. The whole thing could of course only be perfectly, completely accomplished if Peter were alive to understand that Harriet was pregnant, that the child could not possibly be his, and that, if male, would succeed in due course to the Hawkhurst title and estates.

Ideally, according to the Italian code, Peter should die having just learned and understood the significance of that last intelligence. But that was for circumstance to determine; Harriet had not the slightest inclination to embroil herself any further in the matter on grounds so slender, given such a final flourish would be no more than cosmetic, for aesthetic gratification only. Implacable of purpose she may be, but she was not so Italian yet. And besides Fabrizio, she knew, could never be brought to go along with anything of that kind; as a duellist he would kill honourably, but he would never be party to the kind of thing which could have crossed her mind, had she seen fit to allow it to. 'My thought, whose murder yet is but fantastical...' The idea of losing Fabrizio for ever for the sake of what in the end amounted to nothing more than a whim was inconceivable. So, the Peter-Fabrizio thing must take its course as it may, without any involvement on her part. What she had to do was to get to Sebastian as soon as may be.

Harriet knew that it could all work out; she knew the strength of her own purpose; it was all simply a matter of timing. She would monitor the movements of the travelling party from this exquisite place of sojourn with dear friend, Isabella, and plan accordingly.

Dear Cousin Julian, she wrote, *It is now three quarters of one whole year since you departed the shores of England with your charges, and I have resolved to invite you to apprise me, if you will, of your progress so far. I write to Rome, given that, according to your original itinerary, you should be arriving there very soon, if indeed you have not already. I sojourn at Roquebrune, chez my invalid friend, Miss Westlake, at the Villa des Pins. Any correspondence you may feel inclined to address to me should find me here over the next several months, as I bring such comfort and solace as I may to this very dear friend from schooldays whose fortitude in the grip of a malady both progressive and irreversible can elicit nothing but the highest regard and, in me, the most tender affection.*

Having travelled on here from Cousin Sophie at Ménars, I have already heard much of you, both from her and from Charles as well as, more volubly, from the Ménars young men and the little girls, Jeanne and Chantal. I infer from the tone and tenor of their report that your séjour with them was, not to put too fine a point upon it, quite simply a triumph. We too have had our moments of joy together – the hunting and riding around Ménars are a delight; I regret, though, that I was not able to offer the practice at fence, or the instruction at the fisticuffs which featured so prominently, as I understand it, in your time here. And could it really be that Mr Farrell was able to work out possible styles of approach at the knobbly ball game – the jeu du boulet à boules - *always such a cherished favourite at the Château – and explain his reasoning* in French? *Jeanne and Chantal were adamant that 'Edouard nous l'a expliqué en français. Mais si!' And Sophie and Charles made it clear, too, that Edward had featured over your time here as a fine young gentleman and, by implication – completely unwitting of course – not at all the Withybrook oaf I was at such pains to foist upon you. Evidently, Cousin Julian, your influence must have counted for rather*

*more than a mere something, and I have to say that I am
delighted at what I have learned. It always did seem to me
that old Withybrook led that unfortunate boy the most
frightful dance, and that the young man did have much
about him that could be turned to his advantage – witness
his sheer courage, for instance – could his appalling sire
only leave him be and allow him to work out his own
approaches to the world. You have proved me right, I
think, and in doing so rendered a signal service to the
young man. I am indeed avid to view your achievement –
no doubt the estimable Sebastian pursues his equable,
imperturbable, scholarly way? – and à propos, allow
myself to wonder whether we may not rendezvous in the
early autumn, say, somewhere as pleasant as may be
contrived upon your route northwards from Rome? I doubt
if I shall stay in Italy beyond that season now, despite my
original thought of being in Venice for next year's Carnival,
as my dear daughter and her Hawkhurst grandparents
have expressed the wish that I be with them to celebrate
Christmas this year, and I am much inclined to do so. But
I shall remain here with my dearest Isabella for as long as
I may, given the character of her disorder and the strength
of our mutual affection. For the world will indeed be a
wholly different place, once she is no longer of it. Such
desolation, Cousin! Such desolation.*

*Some intelligence, then, vis-à-vis your future projects
would be most welcome. We might aim for a rencontre in
the region of the Lakes, perhaps? Or somewhere more
dramatically mountainous? Such consolation can travel
bring with it! And I suspect, Cousin Julian, that you
yourself are not of so dissimilar a persuasion. Here at
the Villa des Pins we lead a quiet, orderly life. Miss
Westlake it was, you may recall, who first took me into
those fashionable circles of London life in which I
was eventually to meet with Peter de Savigny. Not that
my dear friend is in any way to be held to account for*

that. Over the last twenty years of my life thus far Isabella Westlake has been my closest confidante, adviser and beloved friend, and now that she has need of me, I must be here for her.

Indulge me then, Cousin, with news of your progress and that of your fine protégés. I shall be positively agog with curiosity to see what effects your tour with its enviably multifarious adventures has wrought upon them. And how impressive, that France alone should already have made so signal a contribution, for you are only as yet at the beginning of your Italian 'soggiorno', I think. And Rome! What inordinate good fortune they do enjoy, your young gentlemen, the English 'milordi', as the Ménars girls would insist they were - and I suppose that one day, almost certainly, Mr Farrell will succeed. It has always been my view that Rome should stand as the 'Mecca' of the Tour, which it does, of course, and quite rightly. So here you are, Cousin, on something in the way of a pilgrimage, though I suspect you might take exception to such a notion; let us therefore say rather a journey of appreciation and celebration, as a clear-eyed, unsentimental appraisal, properly informed by knowledge, is surely the highest act of homage to the ancient origins of our latter- day civilisation that it is possible to pay. Oh, for the freedom of your sex to engage in such inspirational enterprises! But I shall desist herewith from further meanderings.

I am, Cousin Julian, your most affectionate, HdeS.

*

In Sienna, Sebastian worked on the notes he had taken as preliminary jottings for his diary entries on Florence.

For a historic city of such proud identity, he wrote,

Florence is a centre positively swarming, it seems, with itinerant English gentry.

In the first instance it was thanks to the Resident, Sir Horace Mann, an acquaintance of my Uncle Greenwood (Can there be anyone of consequence with whom this kinsman is not acquainted?) that we were made known to a range of more or less colourful and eccentric compatriots whose hospitality and good-will towards us became at times well-nigh overwhelming. And it is the eccentricities, I suppose, which remain in the memory, if only because, despite the freedom to roam which the status of independence both implies and confers, one rather expects that gentlemen should be about the business of their estates at home, rather than wandering the continent of mainland Europe in search, frequently, of nothing much more than jejune distraction and dissipation. And oh, the endless round of evenings, mornings, afternoons! Of course people are entitled to take their pleasures as they will; there is nothing more ugly or contemptible to my mind than the self-righteous censure of the puritan conscience. But, to be in Florence and to speak little or nothing of the Italian language? This, surely, is a matter to give one pause.

But of course we did enjoy the sociability, the delicious fare so generously afforded us, more usually than not in exquisite surroundings. After France, and most especially after the hard work of preparation for Italy we took upon ourselves in Provence, it was an amusement to take in the fascinating history of a great city, to revel in the extraordinary beauty of its buildings, gardens, paintings and sculpture.

Only now do I appreciate Uncle Greenwood's thoughts on the châteaux of the Loire being in some sense a foreshadowing of what was in store for us in Italy. In some sense only, I must insist, since nothing in France could possibly have prepared us for such profuse, workaday magnificence as is here. And where else in this old world of ours might one observe a mongrel dog of the streets pissing up against the plinth of a statue by Michelangelo? When the high culture of history, literature, language have given way in the foreground of our recollections to the more urgent concerns which in due course of life may displace them, there will always be the dog in the Piazza della Signoria espied from the Loggia dei Lanzi, the knobbly ball game at Ménars, the truly awesome sight of Maître Courtois at fence with Mr Greenwood, afternoons in a certain shaded room in a quiet corner of Aix-en-Provence.

But we go our respective ways through life; Farrell has his Army career to look forward to, I ?... It is time I set about the business of finding a specific purpose; I cannot live out my days as a creature of passage on the scene of a Florentine conversazione *or whatever, wheresoever. And the circumstances of our Tour have brought me face to face with all this.*

From our vantage point here high above the medieval walls of Sienna, we look out across the rolling countryside of Tuscany, with its vines, its olive-trees and cypresses, and the ancient world beloved of the poets and painters is there, in coexistence with our present time in this year of our Lord, as the convention has it, To promote the continued study and appreciation of that world and the appraisal of its values would be no mean purpose. But it should be in the style of Mr Gibbon, perhaps, rather than in any more direct way. No pedagogue I! I must speak to my Uncle Greenwood about Mr Gibbon; I should so love to make his acquaintance, and I understand he lives in Lausanne. Could that be an attainable destination, on our route northwards?

ROME
(continued)

When they did eventually reach Rome itself after their leisurely progress southwards from Tuscany, they arrived, Julian realised with some vexation, at precisely the wrong time of year, for now the summer was building to its mighty climax. Clearly, it would prove a matter of acute discomfort to venture forth on the kind of projects they might have it in mind to pursue during the best of the sunlight hours.

Privately Julian berated himself furiously. When he had agreed to abandon his Lancashire manor for the best part of two years to take on the responsibilities of the two young men who were neither of them particularly well-known to him, he had quite simply assumed that this major enterprise should be so conducted by himself as to be of lasting profit to them. They should learn the thrill and excitement of such a venture into foreign parts; they should be inspired and edified by new landscapes, the frequent view, in the south, of mountains, the stimulating difference of it all – as he himself had been when, as a young man he too had made his tour. And to that end he had planned as conscientiously as he had ever prepared for a military initiative in his army years. And now he had allowed himself to be caught out where he should not have done. But here the characteristic habit of mind of his army years, instilled during that time of service and never subsequently forgotten, took over. As they would be unable comfortably to negotiate the sights of the great city in the intense heat of the full day, they should adjust their private chronology forward accordingly, so that outings might take place later rather than earlier, life go on into the small hours, with the mornings and the heat of the day for rest and recuperation. Preferably in deep shade, Julian thought wryly. And as it transpired, Sebastian and Edward, after some experience of delicious fare consumed *alfresco* in surroundings of gorgeous historicity, were happy to comply.

The two young men were busy now with tailors and a variety of more or less *louche* individuals, some ostensibly, perhaps even ostentatiously quite grand, who traded in paintings, drawings, prints, sculpture and miscellaneous *objets d'art*. For Edward had received direction from home that he 'might purchase and despatch homewards such embellishments as may fashionably adorn and enhance a nobleman's residence', and the prospect of such novel activity had a particular appeal after the periods of study to which the two of them had so manfully applied themselves.

Edward wondered briefly about his father, where he might have been, what he might have seen or heard to put such an idea into his head.

"The key word being 'fashionably', no doubt", he said to Sebastian, who grinned wickedly.

"The possibilities for a variety of approaches would seem to be... quite a few," he volunteered. "Just consider: 'such embellishments as may fashionably adorn and enhance a nobleman's residence,' eh?"

"Some of Capaldi's stuff might... cause a bit of a stir, don't you think?"

"Oh, definitely. Copulatory explicit? Or mere arousal?"

"My dear Sebastian, Capaldi's arousals are hardly 'mere'!"

"True. But you can't go sticking things like that up all over Warwickshire. Not even you, Nedward."

"Oh, I don't know, you know. How about an 'erotic grotto' by way of forbidden enticement? For the delectation of gentleman only, of course."

"Or gentlemen accompanied by... well, not ladies, anyway - or at least... well?"

"Sebastian! You did not perhaps have someone in mind?"

"No, no, my dear Ned! How could you possibly imagine..."

But Sebastian had been put in mind of Harriet again, a Harriet warmed by wine and reeking of the clandestine cigars she loved so dearly, her eyes bright with drink, desire and mischief, her fingers eager at the waist-band of his breeches, groping downwards, searching...

"It's a marvellous thought, though, isn't it?" asked Edward. "Neddy's den. A secret garden of wicked foreign *erotica*, to outrage the worthy burgesses of Coventry – not that they would ever get the chance to see it, but it could be all the more effective for being nothing more than hearsay - and bring credit and renown, notoriety even, to the name of Withybrook, and of Edward Farrell in particular!"

"Perhaps we should pay a further visit to our egregious friend?"

"Eel Conty? Let us do that. Even if we do end up with nothing more exciting than a brace of Greek athletes, or a modicum of diaphanously draped ladies fiddling with their sandals to show off the full hang of their breasts. And I shall endeavour to possess myself of a modest portfolio of prints and drawings in a certain mode, even if only to titivate the susceptibilities of the noble earl, my parent."

"You'll kill him with the excitement of it, if you do not take care. And Capaldi will *skin* you, Ned."

"He will try to, no doubt."

'Count' Claudio Capaldi traded from a ramshackle edifice in an unremarkable alleyway not far from the Piazza Navona. Oleaginous and dapper – despite grubby cuffs and neck cloth - the Count, as he liked to be known, was a little man who capered and chattered, an untutored maverick of mercurial mind and seemingly inexhaustible vitality whose range of acquaintance and contact stretched far and wide, beyond Italy as well as within it.

Where Capaldi had originated nobody knew; what was undeniable was the fact of his knowledge of the commercial value of paintings, sculpture and *objets d'art,* and his ability to inveigle the 'milordi' of the north into paying what were no doubt exorbitant prices for the pieces he sold them, pieces acquired through an extensive if shadowy net-work of agents operating on his behalf out of Rome and elsewhere. One had the feeling that Capaldi would not be over scrupulous about the provenance of his wares, provided there was nothing to implicate him in any kind of equivocal dealings over acquisition.

There was, decidedly, something of the fence about Capaldi, one who ran a dark empire by dint of persuasions one would rather not inquire too closely into. But the 'milordi' were lavish with money and eager to make their purchases. Capaldi's people would of course see to all the irksome details of package and despatch homewards. Edward Farrell was reminded of old Timothy Kydd back in London, for they were two of a kind, Kydd and Capaldi. Of a kind to be found in any major city in the world – hungry, avid for wealth or consequence, ruthless to those who served them, solitaries whose longing to belong had impelled them into positions of a kind of real dominance, like the crippled leader of a street gang who terrorised underlings more hale and hearty than himself. It had however been made clear to Edward and Sebastian by more than one English acquaintance with whom they had spoken of such matters that, in Rome, Capaldi was the man to find you virtually anything you might ask him to. They therefore made a number of sallies into the environs of the great city, to stroll through gardens of exquisitely picturesque villas at Tivoli, Genzano and else-where in order to note the kind of thing they might take it into their heads to purchase and ship home. Julian, about his own occasions, left them to it; they should prosper or founder in this one by themselves and of their own accord. "Just beware, gentlemen, what you get into," he had said, "the dealer's world can be fraught with hazard; there are 'sharp' characters afoot, and I would not have either of you take a stiletto in the ribs some dark night in some noisome alleyway. Can I make any inquiries on your behalf?"

"Not for the moment, sir, thank you."

So they pursued their excursions and wanderings - to the Villa d'Este, the Farnesina, the Medici and others – acquiring in the process something of the geography of the city and its environs, and no little appreciation of the art of the garden in Italy.

"I'll have a garden, too," said Ned one evening as they cantered in leisurely style back into the city and home. "I mean, I'll have one constructed to my design, from prints and things. And the naughty bit shall be... *concealed,* with a secret entrance beyond the maze, an entrance known probably only to me, so that those invited at my discretion shall gibber and slobber themselves into near distraction if they try to find it for themselves a second time on their own. Yes, I like the idea of that."

"Farrell, this is... not proper. You aim to strike at men by exploiting their... vulnerabilities."

"That is the notion, yes. But Sebastian, this is nothing new, is it? I'd wager old Hadrian knew a thing or two, there; the Romans did, you know."

As he listened to his friend, Sebastian recalled the stoa, the pool and gardens at the villa of that emperor, and also the terrible image of the Colosseum, with its appalling, only too imaginable cruelties.

"The use of desire as a weakness to be exploited in games of dominance? No, I suppose it is not new," he said, "but I never imagined you to be so taken with such things. Beyond the thought of a gratifying fuck, I mean."

"Neither did I, my philosophic friend, so perhaps it is one of the things, the many things I have learned even thus far, during the course of this Tour? But consider, Sebastian, the irony of it; the 'fashionable adornments' of Neddy's Den become a household word – or a whispered word, more likely – in the great houses of England. I might even induce Royals to visit, one day!"

"I thought you aspired to military command, Farrell, not to the position of Pornographer Royal."

"That above all, sir. The rest is... no more than the amusement of an idle moment. But one may indulge the fancy a little, eh? And the idea of an Inspector General of Cavalry on his hands and knees in all his finery, gobbling and pleading to be allowed another look!…"

"Just provided, *mon cher ami,* that such indulgences do not lead one into either disease, discredit, destitution or death. Death either immediate or eventual, I might add."

"The pox?"

"Precisely. And you might also care to recall, as you go after your 'particular treasures', that Italians are traditionally expert, and probably still are, at subtle means of extermination,painful or otherwise. Poisons and things, Farrell. Fascinating, don't you think?"

"I do not. I much prefer a good mill, face to face with an honest adversary."

"No doubt. But that is not the accustomed way with these people. So beware, old Nedward."

"Be reassured, Sebastian. I shall set myself a definite limit. A reasonable limit."

"Then be sure not to disclose it, for knowing that, Capaldi would surely endeavour to take you beyond it." Sebastian was momentarily reminded of the truly enormous wealth his friend commanded, and was suddenly anxious for him.

"Yes, Sebastian. I had anticipated something of the sort. One does, you know."

*

Back at the lodgings, shuttered and shaded from the Roman afternoon, Julian Greenwood was writing a reply to the letter from Cousin Harriet at Roquebrune.

…it would therefore be most disingenuous on my part, he wrote, *not to   allow that I was gratified and not a little flattered, even, by your observations on what you   had inferred of our effect – if that is appropriate – upon the*

*household of Sophie and Charles at Ménars. Certainly
the young men hit it off immediately in capital style –
Philippe and Aurélien were already of course not unknown
to Sebastian, although their first acquaintance had taken
place some years previously – and I have to say that it was
largely in consequence of the spirited mutual sympathy
engendered from the first moment of our arrival that both
my gentlemen made such huge progress in their mastery
of the French language. Sebastian did in fact spend much
of his time with Sophie; their tastes for literature, music
and the telling of stories seemed wholly congruent, and
Sebastian was of course given the freedom of Sophie's
modest but discriminating library. And where more pleasant
than that exquisite, panelled corner turret room in the
château to while away an hour or two with Ronsard, Du
Bellay, La Fontaine...?*

*Mr Farrell learned in an altogether more practical
manner, over swordplay, pugilism and also, at the
irresistible insistence of the little girls, whose total failure
to appreciate the sheer difficulty involved in acquiring any
language other than ones own meant that Edward –
'Edouard!' – was obliged to find ways of making his
meanings intelligible to them. For the Honourable Mr
Farrell has a heart which is not unsusceptible to the
blandishments of young females – whether intended or, as
in this case, merely instinctive if not entirely guileless –
and he found himself in honour and chivalry bound to
find solutions to the kind of problems he had previously
encountered only in the arid pages of text books which
had never been of more than scant interest to him. A fine
young man, away from the dominance of his parent – one
who has never impressed me one iota on the few occasions
upon which I have found myself in his proximity in London.*

However, nous voici enfin à Rome, pour ainsi dire! *We
have at last reached - in a period of just under a
twelvemonth – that great city which cannot but be the focus*

and singular magnet of a Tour such as this is. So, although I have to say that I am inclined to cut down on the excessive viewing of churches - the assertive presence of the Roman Church over the landscapes of this mainland of Europe I find offensive enough - we have made a start to our duties with the ancient centre - Forum, Circus Maximus, Colosseum. We understand too, I think, how the spiritual empire of the Roman Church was renewed by ambitious popes some two hundred years or so ago, give or take a decade or two, in such a way as to emulate as it surpassed the secular might of ancient Rome - just ponder the significance of all those Alexanders, Caesars, Juliuses! And we hack our way across the landscapes of a hundred paintings, to view gardens, villas, ruins; truly we are becoming cognoscenti of the picturesque. We visit acquaintances and take up previous introductions; we toy with the notion of purchase - of sculpture, statuary, prints and paintings to be later installed and displayed in embellishment of our northern places. And I do have to say that the idea of a fine Italian garden at the Warwickshire residence of a noble English earl - for such one day Edward will surely be - does have an appeal of its own particular kind. Sebastian, of course, finds more to interest him on a smaller scale - in paintings, bronze statuettes, tapestries, less than gigantic in their dimensions. He was, I know, greatly, lastingly impressed by the Cellini statuettes at Azay-le-Rideau; they are frequently in his mind.

So, Mr Farrell shall become the collector, Mr Haverhill the connoisseur, and both in their respective ways stand to gain very significantly from this experience of foreign civilisation. I guide and advise, of course, but to profit from a tour such as this is one must find the impulse to do so from deep within oneself. Sebastian is fortunately of a naturally philosophic disposition; Mr Farrell is a more interesting case, in that he had to find good and immediate cause for his efforts.   He was fortunate in doing precisely that, first through the sympathy and generosity of his own cousins in Paris, the Châtignys – with whom you have, I think, some acquaintance through your friend, Geneviève d'Aubignac and her family – and subsequently through the manly bonhomie of Philippe and Aurélien de Ménars, as well as through the unremitting insistence on intelligible answers to questions from Jeanne and Chantal, who proved quite unable to at this stage of their lives to see him as anything other than a Frenchman who, for unaccountable reasons – and quite probably gratuitously perverse ones – persisted in speaking an unintelligible language of his own since he found it difficult, to begin with, to express himself in French.   Clearly, Charles and Sophie made the decision not to confuse their children by attempting to raise them in two languages simultaneously. No doubt they will learn English eventually, but they will always speak with an accent now – not that that is of any great import; a French accent among ladies of fashion is not unacceptable, I believe.

Returning to Edward however, it was he, I confirm, who painstakingly worked out the descriptions of throwing or pitching techniques for the knobbly ball game, such a foolishly engaging affair which I recall with affection from my own earlier times at Ménars.   Rather like penning the rules of cricket in French, would you not agree?

Dearest Harriet, write to me again, if you will, on the subject of a rendezvous, somewhere by the northern Lakes, perhaps?   Or close by mountains?   For it would be a true pleasure to renew our acquaintance during the course of these travels.   And cherish your sick friend, my dear Cousin.   For while passion may come and go, friendship, if it is genuine, will endure and grace the lives of those fortunate enough to find and value it as it should be valued...

To one such as myself, wrote Sebastian Haverhill, *steeped since childhood in the letters and civilisation of Latin antiquity, the experience of this great city of Rome comes, as it were, almost as* déjà vu. *Not, certainly, in the style of an English lady of our acquaintance at home to whom it was immediately apparent, on her first visit to Florence, that she had been there before, given the wholly unanticipated familiarity with which she found herself able to make her way about the streets and squares of that unique place, but rather as a confirmation – in the real terms of what is ordinary and everyday – of what one knew already, or sensed, at least, from the kind of inferences one is encouraged to make from the reading of Latin texts. For, despite the ostensible muddle and confusion of the palimpsest face of this city today, it is possible to contrive – however much by virtue of artifice – the timeless view of particular aspects. One may compose, for instance, in the manner of a painter, an exclusive view of a stone fountain or garden feature, where water flows from the open mouth of an ancient visage; one may view the ruins of antiquity and engineer particular angles of sight so as to exclude the general ruination; one may contemplate a Renaissance villa bracketed by umbrella pines – deep green against ochre walls – in a manner calculated to highlight the historical actuality of a view designed to be outside of time. Such impressions will, I think, remain among the myriad fragments of that totality which shall be my memory of Rome. For, just as the notion of 'Rome' is so huge in its ramifications as to be quite beyond any comprehensive, all inclusive sense of a whole, so this great city, equally vast in detail and feature, is simply not to be possessed by such travellers in transit as we are, from within the momentary compass of a modest and all too brief sojourn.*

Farrell is busy arranging for his purchase of statuary

et alia *to be created up and conveyed to England. It appears, as we surmised, that Capaldi has ways of seeing to such matters, for which no doubt he will charge the old Ned hugely. But Farrell is of course inordinately wealthy, and the delight he shall derive from the arranging of his den, grotto, or secret garden will more than justify the expense incurred in acquisition and transportation. It does just occur to me to wonder how he imagines he might square the pagan delights of his private* erotica *with the proper Catholic modesty of his sweet Châtigny cousin, Mademoiselle Clothilde – not, sadly, that he is ever likely to wish to display them to her, given the likely bent of his father's prejudice concerning that persuasion.*

In a matter of weeks we shall be leaving for the north. But we do still have Naples, Venice and the Lakes to look forward to, and I understand my Uncle Greenwood has further acquaintance he is anxious to pursue – when has he not? – here in Rome, this time in German circles known to him from correspondence and his own previous times of residence in 'Germania'. Probably Ned and I shall not be much part of that, not here in Rome, anyway. But the German perspective will afford yet another novel view to add to our already extensive portfolio of such things; it will also afford something in the way of an anticipation of what is yet to come in the latter phase of our travels. And, sated as I am, I do still long for more.

ITALIAN CAPRICE
Part Three

SEBASTIAN HAVERHILL
1885

In the exquisite, calf-bound volumes of my Grandfather's diaries of the Tour, *Sebastian Haverhill: a Grand Tour of Foreign Parts 1785-87,* the record of the travellers' continuing progress is to be found - to Naples, where they made the acquaintance through that capable mentor, Julian Greenwood Esquire, of a distinguished circle of German residents which included the lady, Angelika Kaufmann, her fellow painter Wilhelm Tischbein and, most distinguished of all to be, the Herr Geheimrat Wolfgang von Goethe, now justifiably revered by the *cognoscenti* as one of our European world's greatest literary geniuses. Among my Grandfather's literary effects there exists a further calf-bound volume, also privately printed, which is considerably more slender than the three fat tomes of Tour reminiscence; it comprises an account cum monographic study of the achievements, character and thought of one of whom my Grandfather clearly found himself in some awe. There is correspondence, too, with reference to subsequent occasional meetings, in Weimar and elsewhere, which took place virtually up to the time of the death of this great *savant* and German gentleman of letters in 1832.

Mr Farrell had found, it seems to me, that the French stage of the Tour had been and would remain what was most preciously and vividly alive in his memory, given that it did become for him a recollection of all those things which had contributed to his personal formation. And indeed, from an irascible young oaf somewhat too quick to take offence and back himself with fisticuffs, he did develop into the polished military aristocrat whose possibilities our great-great Uncle Greenwood had depicted – with rare imagination – for him. My Grandfather however, despite the spectacular grandeurs of Rome which had seemed so overwhelming at the time, found himself most particularly affected in the longer term by the latter part of the Tour, post-France, post-Italy, spent in Dresden and Berlin.

There is more to say of Mr Farrell, and much of a poignantly private and even tragic nature, and I shall return to him in due course, but for the moment my Grandfather Sebastian shall be the focus of my concern.

From Naples the travellers made an unforgettable excursion to the Greek site at Paestum where, my Grandfather notes, the marvellous aesthetics of the temple architecture there put the Romans, for him, unequivocally into a perspective of inferiority. For all their worldly greatness, their achievements in law, engineering, politics and administration, the Romans remain firmly earth-bound, where those temples proffered intimations of a perfection belonging to a realm beyond the concrete, to that region of ideal forms adumbrated by the philosopher, Plato. And oh, how the heart does lift at the recollection of ones first sight of them, so vividly recaptured in my Grandfather's account! *'It is almost',* he writes, *'as if one had been afforded a glimpse of the lineaments of an eternal cosmic proportion, and one which would endure outside of time itself, given the absolute and axiomatic truth of what it made manifest.'* The temples at Paestum may have been erected – ostensibly at least – to the greater glory of ancient gods; what they celebrate in fact is mathematics.

So classic Greek concerns marry into a perspective of last century where human capability was more or less tacitly held to be the measure of everything that gave value to existence. And it may well have been this which eventually drew my Grandfather into his life-long study of the great German writers of the Enlightenment, the *Aufklärung,* once he had acquired yet another language, the German, to add to his Latin, his French and his Italian.

Such, at least, are the inferences which I draw from the observations of my Grandfather as he noted them at that time, in the autumn of 1786. I did remark at the beginning of this work of mine how, with my Grandfather and myself, affinity seemed to have skipped a generation, that I had always found myself more in sympathy with his view of things than with that of my father Edward, named after my Grandfather's boon companion of the Tour.

The Honourable Edward Farrell, later fifth Earl of Withybrook and distinguished commander of cavalry, followed a military career of dashing exploit and great daring, spanning some twenty-seven years of continuous service during which his relentless, implacable pursuit of the French had at times seemed to those who cared for him to verge on the insane and suicidal. For this Lord Withybrook, who never married, had cherished over those years a private misery and despair which, beneath that polished, brilliant exterior, had led him close to the most appalling degradations which might easily have brought him to ruin and worse, had it not been for the loving concern of my Grandfather, who had stood by him through the worst of his living agonies. For Edward Farrell, the soldier, the possibility of death in action must surely have been the cleanest end of which he could have dreamed, or even prayed for.

My father, Edward Haverhill, who in his generation died in his command at Sebastopol forty years after the great Duke had finally settled scores with Bonaparte, found his affinity most likely with his dashing namesake and god-father, and with my great-Grandfather, Simon Haverhill, veteran of the American War, who is so amusingly noted by his son as being quite out of sympathy with the *milieux* frequented by Mrs de Savigny, Mr Greenwood and their like, 'where people never quite mean what they say, dammit!'

And my mention here of Mrs de Savigny puts me in mind of further matters of interest where the historical context of my Grandfather's Tour is concerned. For there was a meeting, somewhere east of Lake Garda, as the travellers made their way northwards from Rome, towards Venice first, then on up to the mountains and over the Julian Alps into Austria. And it must have taken place most likely, this *rencontre,* somewhere in the region of the Euganean Hills, just below the triangle formed by Verona, Vicenza and Padua; a rendezvous and reunion apparently first proposed by Harriet de Savigny in a letter she had written from her dying friend's house at Roquebrune to Julian Greenwood. Which brings me close to matters of some delicacy – albeit not altogether bereft of the possibilities of high comedy, not to mention even knockabout farce. As follows:

In the early autumn of 1787 Harriet de Savigny gave birth, in London, to a male heir to the Hawkhurst title and estates. Prior to this event, as its imminence became apparent, the lady had contrived to intimate to some few among her London acquaintance rather given, as it happened, to gossip, that there had indeed been a short-lived *rapprochement* between herself and the appalling Peter in Italy the previous winter. However, from the very mentions – brief, contemptuous, dismissive - of Harriet's wayward husband noted by poor Isabella Westlake in the private diaries unearthed by myself from amongst my mother's her cousin's effects from the time of her death, it does seem unlikely, indeed quite incredible that Harriet de Savigny should have given herself to Peter as a wife again in the necessary way for that child to have been conceived.

I do know that my Grandfather Sebastian had always entertained the greatest affection for his brilliant Aunt Harriet, and that her interest in him, as the devilishly handsome young gentleman he must surely have been at the time, had long been very decidedly less than proper. But then, such things were hardly uncommon among families of the upper class in those so much more easy-going days. So, my conclusion should be obvious, and if this, strictly speaking, can be no more than conjecture, I insist that the thoughts and ways and sentiments of my Grandfather are quite simply so familiar to me after my close study over the years of everything he wrote – whether in English or in the German language – as far as is known, that the truth of the matter cannot be other than this. Somewhere along that route northwards, Harriet contrived a *rencontre* with our travellers in order that she might use a no doubt willing and virile young Sebastian Haverhill to father the future Lord Hawkhurst. And if this is indeed the case, then for once the fates did smile upon the fortunes of Harriet de Savigny, when her disinherited and hopelessly dissipated husband was despatched in mid-1787 by a villainous but timely and expert dagger thrust to the eye in the course of some squalid broil in a gaming house cum brothel somewhere in the stews of Vienna.

In her subsequent day Harriet de Savigny was of course one of the great beauties of the fashionable world; in her earlier days at the time of her marriage to Peter de Savigny she had been noted by many an envious young gentleman of society as a lady of exceptional and no doubt erotic charisma. Whatever the truth of that matter, she was undoubtedly a lady of energy and spirit, and one who must have coped with some degree of resilience with the pain of her situation once the unspeakable Savigny had abandoned her. Thus it is that I have it in mind to believe that she might well have planned her second pregnancy as, for one thing, an act of revenge against Peter, who was to have been left to writhe for the rest of his miserable days in the bitterness of the knowledge that the heir to those estates, title and fortune which should have been his was not his son. It would have been an appropriately Italian style of revenge. I have of course no means of knowing whether this had or had not been Harriet's planned intention. At all events the untimely demise of the awful Savigny did preclude any enjoyment of so exquisite a retribution. In the days, not so distant still, when offenders were hanged and drawn before quartering, the expert practitioner, it is said, could work so fast and so skilfully at his grisly purposes that he was able to show his victim his own heart and entrails before life was finally extinguished. Savigny was at least spared an equivalent ignominy.

*

My Grandfather's diary account of the journey northwards from Lake Garda - after Venice, the final, crowning sojourn of the Italian stage of the Tour – to Trento, into the Alto Adige and eventually up to the Brenner Pass and into Austria concerns itself to a considerable extent with the huge distances covered and the monotony of the road, relieved only by reading deliberately chosen to be of so absorbing a kind as to distract attention from the discomfort of the journey and the necessary boredom of the travellers' situation.

They had covered France in relatively easy stages, with long breaks between their various stints on the highways of that country. Now they urged it upon themselves and their hapless coachmen to put large tracts of distance behind them, and with some despatch, in order that they might cross the mountains and make their way with all the alacrity of a Julian Greenwood now eager to renew his acquaintance with the German friends who awaited them. And by now, with so much in the way of experience afforded them by the Tour thus far, the young men did find themselves better equipped mentally to cope with the exigencies of the journey.

In this next extract from his diaries, my Grandfather attempts to marshal his thoughts and feelings as they prepare to bid farewell to Italy after that final, marvellous stop in Carnival Venice:

Probably we lingered an excessive time in and around Rome, he writes, *because, although this is something which may be easily understood, it meant that we did have to cut short our time here in order to maintain the momentum of our progress northwards. I do not propose to write at length about Venice yet, other than to note, for future reference, that after the grandeur of Rome the magnificent idiosyncrasy of that incomparable island – with all its gorgeous manifestations of a proud eccentricity combined with a worldly determination to maintain a pre-eminence which did endure over centuries – will surely remain, for me, one of the truly great features of the Tour. But more of Venice after due reflection. Tomorrow we make our way up into the mountains and by way of the Brenner Pass over the summits and down into Austria, the first of the German-speaking lands.*

So, this is finally good-bye to Italy, and to all that it represents of the brilliant South. For it is truly a land of fabulous content, this Italy, with its colour and its splendour and its spectacular manifestations of a historical past which, viewed for the first time and never to be forgotten, lives on in its vigorous everyday reminders of what was, and of what we have known about from our own earliest days. For we have gazed upon the lineaments of classical antiquity without which, certainly, the world we inhabit would have been a very different place.

The gradual approach to the mountains, as they loom larger and larger over several days of progress up the highway to the north, does prepare one, I suppose, for the inevitable, imminent leave-taking. What a pity we have as yet no English poet to celebrate the splendour of Italy with us, as we settle into our fire-side chairs to sit out the worst of our northern winters as cosily as we may. (Happily my Grandfather did live long enough to enjoy much of the work of Mr Browning who, clearly, is the sort of poet he must have had in mind when he penned these thoughts all those years ago; happily too, he refrained from retrospective revisions of this text, for had he not done so it would have lost much of its spontaneous value as a historical piece. SH 1885)

Certainly I myself was afforded much opportunity for reflection upon all that wealth of experience which had been ours in the Latin world of France and Italy. My dear old Ned too, I noted, was silent and even thoughtful for much of the time, although it is never easy to read Ned's thoughts on anything; he invariably appears, and largely by deliberate design now, in so pragmatic and non-speculative a light.

My Uncle Greenwood, I know, is looking forward to renewing yet more of his extensive acquaintance in the German lands. It has been a feature of this Tour – and not the least impressive of features at that – how very much at home he is able to make himself wherever we may be. And indeed, there is something there for Ned the Guards Officer to be to take note of, as my Uncle Greenwood has been at pains to point out most specifically and explicitly for his edification. And how would Ned have fared on campaign without such preliminary advice? One can hardly imagine his own parent taking the analytical, thoughtful line on how to survive in reasonable comfort so as to be of use to ones commanders and ones men in the field. And yet, one could hardly command effectively if one were in pain or discomfort, if one were exhausted or starving. My Uncle Greenwood, I surmise, has rendered Ned the most signal service in the way he has tutored him and coaxed his imagination into a larger sense of purpose than one might have thought possible. So, each of us with his own thoughts, we prepare to bid farewell to Italy, as we depart for the ascent of the pass tomorrow. Shall one ever return, one wonders? Inevitably, one must wonder, given the vast distances we travel to reach these parts in the first place.

The mountains too do have their own kind of appeal, for they are a powerful, unforgettable feature of the scene over much of the mainland of Europe. Indeed, one is hardly aware, if aware at all, as an islander, what a very important Aspect of that mainland they are, together with the forests, lakes and rivers - especially the great rivers. And I recall too how very impressed we were from the first by the Loire and, later, the Rhone. Now we look forward to our first sight of the legendary Danube, and subsequently the Rhine its very self, the mightiest of all, with its robber castles set high on crags above the water, and the huge barges, reduced to toy size from that vantage point, that ply its highway below. Such at least is what one is led to believe of it, from the drawings and illustrations of earlier travellers. And such a sight will truly be something to look forward to with keen anticipation, something to carry away as yet another exquisite memory of the latter part of the Tour, as it takes us into the German lands.

A further thought occurs. Having timed our all too brief sojourn in Venice to coincide with Carnival -that mad riot of the most spectacular colours, masks and costumes it is possible to imagine (and how those colours do seem to work their liberating effect upon the fantasy!)- we leave Italy and make for the north just as the first intimations of Spring begin to make themselves manifest here, as the chill of the earliest months of this new year, 1787, gives way to that softer, more balmy atmosphere which heralds the onset of Italy's bright summer. And I anticipate that the chill of the darker seasons will still hold sway in the mountains, and that our travels beyond them shall lead us, the further north we go, back –as it were– into winter. What we leave behind is, therefore, a fairy-land of unforgettable marvels, the whole warmly contained within the glow of the strength of the sun and the radiance of its light. That being so, how can one possibly bring oneself to leave at all? It would, I surmise, be the easiest thing imaginable to forgo the latter part of the Tour in the interest of a more protracted residence in this lovely land. But we shall, with our northern sense of purpose, maintain the progress of our itinerary. The answer shall therefore be to return...

*

Ironically, in view of this, the next and final stages of the Tour proved, for my Grandfather, to be the most abiding in their influence upon the development of his thought, and the most signal in the indications they afforded him of a possible direction for his purposes. As follows: My Grandfather, Sebastian Haverhill, became over subsequent years a name to be noted and held in high regard for those writings in which he interpreted and commented upon the literature and scholarship of certain German writers and *savants* of our own time, in his later life, having made a start, in his earlier years, with some key figures from the previous century.

For the Germany into which the travellers now made their way in the Spring of 1787 was a Germany which had much to offer where scholarship and innovative, adventurous thought was concerned, and much of this Enlightenment deliberation did have to do with the significance of the ancient world for modern, contemporary times.

À propos of all this, however, I should make the point here that it has always seemed to me that the Latin writer Tacitus, so revered amongst historians, did in fact do little service to our study of the past with his notion of 'Germania', for inevitably the concept of a German unity does postulate something which until very recently has not corresponded to the actuality of things where the German-speaking lands are concerned. And although Tacitus was scrupulous enough in his efforts to ascribe more or less exact geographical locations for the German tribes of his day, so out-landish are the names of these that it would take one much more learned than I can claim to be in the history and historical lore of those parts to identify anything there that might be of contemporary significance. What remains from Tacitus is unequivocally an impression of a kind of unity, of homogeneity, where over the ages none has existed.

Consider, by way of example, the itinerary of the Greenwood travelling party. From the Brenner Pass they make their way through the Austrian Tyrol to Munich, capital of the kingdom of Bavaria. They then cross the Danube at Passau, an independent Bishopric, into Bohemia and Slavic land for a momentary sojourn at Prague, that magical city which later that same year was to be graced by the incomparable Mozart for the premiere of his opera, Don Giovanni, at the recently constructed Tyl Theatre. From Prague they continue northwards and into Saxony, its own kingdom, where they reside awhile in exquisite, baroque Dresden before proceeding northwards again to Berlin, where Edward Farrell, duly advised by Mr Greenwood, was able to consider and observe the formidable Prussian military machine created by three generations of Hohenzollern kings.

At the same time, the Berlin of 1787, less than twelve months on from the death of that complex figure, Frederick the Great, was a place where French modes ruled in fashionable society; it was also a centre of learning – and destined in our own time to become an even greater one – of art and of music, this latter being a particularly gracious, gratifying German addiction.

So it happened that my Grandfather, now perfectly at home in the French language which was the accepted vehicle of discourse in polite Berlin circles and no doubt encouraged by Mr Greenwood, found himself sufficiently intrigued by the German language to set about learning it, and thus adding to his already considerable store. That part of his diary which covers the period of their time in Berlin affords something in the way of one clue as to how this may, at least in part, have been brought about.

The other day, having been resident in this extraordinary city for the best part of a fortnight, we were bidden to dine at the elegant home of a certain Monsieur Steinberg, a Berlin gentleman of affairs and old acquaintance of my Uncle Greenwood. There was to be music and entertainment of the soirée salon kind, and as Mr Greenwood was eager to renew relations with his old friend so we, equally, were curious to witness the kind of social

*gathering which quite manifestly featured as typical of
cultivated circles in so brilliant a milieu. For truly, Berlin
– the city of the Bear, no less! – is a place of vitality and
elegance, the latter of course being very much in the French
style of things. It did also occur to me that my Uncle
Greenwood might well be as interested in the present
condition of the city, and indeed of Prussia as a whole, as
he had shown himself to be in the condition of France at
the outset of this Tour.*

*So we made our way to the Steinberg residence, where
we found somewhat to our relief that the outlandish, native
family names of these Brandenburgers, Prussians and
Saxons were invariably preceded by forenames in their
French formulation, so one was able to address the
daughters of the family, of whom there were several, as
Mademoiselle Charlotte, Mademoiselle Jeannette, and so
on.*

*Farrell, to his delight, found some officers to talk to –
fine, proud, manly fellows who soon put off their hauteur
when they learned he was destined for the Guards; he
was quickly engaged in lively conversation with these
gentlemen and, my Uncle Greenwood being equally taken
up elsewhere, I found myself – not unwillingly –
appropriated by the daughters of the family as ' Monsieur
Sébastien' who insisted I be part of their circle and party
to their chatter. By this time we were drinking tea and
happily conversing in the French tongue, which they all
seemed to speak with considerable flair. Then, quite
unexpectedly, the use of phrase in the native language
sent them all off into fits of giggles, until my obvious
puzzlement drew immediate sympathy from these kind-
hearted, pleasant young ladies. One of them, Mademoiselle
Jeannette, was nominated to be, as it were, go-between in
the matter of languages, and to explain to their bemused
English guest what might be in question.*

Thus it was that I found myself listening to the most

extraordinary tale recounted in the German language –
with what were quite clearly dialectal embellishments and
switches of accent to characterise the principal figures in
the story, a wonderful, heart- warming story of kings, and
wood-cutters, and frogs and forests, and magical
transformations of a whole variety of kinds. It was
explained to me that they had such stories not from books,
but by word of mouth from nursemaids, nannies and
household servants. 'They belong to the people, you see,
Monsieur. Old Gretel in the kitchen knows hundreds,
absolutely hundreds,' said Mademoiselle Sophie, the
youngest of the sisters and cousins. 'Papa is not too happy
about our listening to them and repeating them. "Ladies,"
he maintains, "should speak French." But who, Monsieur,
could resist such enchanting tales?'

'Who indeed?' said I. And I was put in mind of that
volume of Provençal tales which we had come across at
the antiquarian's shop in Aix-en-Provence, and was able
to tell them of it, and to recount the gist of 'The Bishop
and the Giant Worm'. And it was there and then that it
occurred to me, even as I engaged in such happy
conversation with my enchanting young hostesses, that
such stories must surely exist in abundance all over Europe
– unrecorded, passed on, unlike the great literary oeuvres
which derive from classical antiquity, by word of mouth
only, in almost every language and dialect of the continent.
And it occurred to me also that there may well be a very
considerable number of these, belonging to, say, remote,
mountain places of which I had never even heard. The
thought was a sobering one, as it dawned upon me that,
despite all the work I had put in on the Latin, French and
Italian languages, there remained still a huge treasure there
that was, as yet, still wholly unknown to me – of all sorts
and kinds of marvellous things.

'Monsieur is looking very thoughtful', remarked one
of the ladies, a mischievous sixteen-year old with a truly

wicked glint in her bright blue eyes.

'I am thinking,' said I, 'that I should like to know more of your wonderful tales.'

'Then you must begin, Monsieur, by learning the German language.'

'And we shall begin,' said Mademoiselle Charlotte, the eldest of the sisters, by teaching you that the word for 'conte', fairy-tale in German, is 'Märchen'.

Listen carefully, Monsieur, for you will not be familiar with this 'ch' sound. 'Märchen'.'

'Märchen', said I, and all applauded my very first German word. Then we fell by a kind of tacit mutual agreement into a companionable riot of happy giggles.

'And what might all that have been about?' asked Ned later, as we made our way back to our lodgings. 'Giggling away with all those ladies, I saw you, Sebastian.' Ned was happy, expansive and at ease with himself after his military stint with the young officers; men of very much his own age and kind. Perhaps he had been afforded a glimpse of his own future – something to look forward to after the inevitable anticlimax of our return to England.

'Oh, old folk-tales in the German language. The ladies learn them from their servants and nurses.'

'Do they now? I don't imagine Papa is too happy about that, is he?'

'Apparently not,' said I, ' but they ignore him. And the tales are simply wonderful.'

'And how would you know that?'

'They told me several. Translated into French. But this language, the German I mean, does intrigue me. I think I shall have to learn it.'

'Ah!' said Mr Greenwood, and I caught the glint of understanding and sympathy in his eye, and knew that he had perceived my curiosity and approved of it.

ITALIAN CAPRICE
Part Four
Afterword

SEBASTIAN HAVERHILL
1885

Over subsequent years my Grandfather did acquire an extensive and expert knowledge of the German language and become an authoritative literary commentator in two quite separate fields. The first of these concerned the Enlightenment, and the renewal of interest in the ancient world among German scholars which was attributable to the efforts of such as Winckelmann, Klopstock, Lessing and others leading inevitably to Schiller and Goethe. And here my Grandfather's thorough grounding in Latin, his knowledge of Italian, his enduring love of Roman Italy and his familiarity with that country in many of its ancient and Renaissance aspects combined with his more recent acquisition of the German tongue to enable him to look with understanding and sympathy upon the enthusiasm and purposes of those outstanding scholars and writers who had made it their business to bring the brilliant culture of the ancient Mediterranean fresh to the minds of their northern contemporaries. And one can imagine what a matter of pride it must have been to him to find himself in a position to read the magisterial 'Italian Journey' of his friend, Herr von Goethe, in the language of its composition within only a few years of its appearance.

In his deep and scholarly love of Italy, although that did focus primarily upon the ancient world of Rome, my Grandfather fulfilled the role, as it were, of a post-Enlightenment precursor for English readers to Mr Browning, albeit with nothing, it has to be said, of the mercurial dash and style of that accomplished poet. Thus the first business of my

Grandfather's life became the scholarly interpretation of the Enlightenment thought of the authors already mentioned, and it was not until considerably later in his days that he developed the second, abiding fascination of his German interest when he became the first English translator of the fairy-tales of the brothers Grimm over the earlier decades of the present century.

Thus it was that, as a very old man, my Grandfather did receive the honour of signal approval from Albert of Saxe-Coburg, German Prince Consort to our present lady sovereign for his thoughtful, sustained contribution to mutual understanding between the two countries. For myself, I am convinced – or, it pleases me to think – that this life-long fascination of his with the folk-tales of the German speaking peoples provided him perhaps with a welcome refuge from happy recollections of the French experience of the Tour so irreversibly marred and outraged by the events of the Revolution in that country – of which more shortly. It pleases me also to think that that fascination, running alongside his scholar's affection for the then so novel deliberations of the Enlightenment writers, may well have had its origins in that exchange between the young Sebastian Haverhill, 'a devilish handsome young fellow, if ever there was one', as my great, great Uncle Greenwood once so aptly put it, and those spirited young German ladies *chez Steinberg* in the far distant Berlin of 1787. For thus are seeds of great value sown in the casual, good-natured flirtations of engaging young people. And did my Grandfather Sebastian, one wonders, ever look back with happy nostalgia to that memorable *soirée* with the Mesdemoiselles Steinberg? I do like to surmise that he must surely have done so.

In the year of the Battle of Trafalgar, my Grandfather, then aged forty, was married to a lady of the West Country somewhat younger than himself, one Miss Anna Richards – surprisingly enough, given his intellectual propensities, a daughter of the Church, since her father was an archdeacon in the diocese of Wells. In the course of time several children were born to this union, of whom the eldest was my own father, Edward, named after the life-long friend and boon if unlikely companion of his father's Grand Tour, and like whom he eventually pursued a military career in his god-father's regiment. And I have no doubt that Edward, fifth Earl of Withybrook, did find the time between the unceasing campaigns of his hectic, driven, military existence to instruct the little boy in certain essentials such as riding to hounds, swordplay and fisticuffs. For, given the endearingly contradictory character of Edward Farrell, it is easy enough to imagine this elegant colonel of Life Guards brawling with his friend's son with some considerable relish, and to hear my Grandfather's deliberately pained exasperation in the query:

"Farrell, you look as though you actually enjoy *this kind of thing. Can this be so?"* And Ned's reply: *"Most certainly, man. And next year we shall be after the fox together, shall we not, Edward?"* A moment of true contentment and happiness, one would hope, if all too brief. For the life of Edward Farrell, fifth Earl of Withybrook, after the ending of the Tour, had been beset by the most dreadful misfortune.

In the Summer of 1789, two years almost after the travellers' return to England, the Chateau de Ménars was burned to the ground, the family murdered on the doorstep of *la maison* by one of the many drunken mobs which, at the time of the Great Fear, *la Grande Peur,* ravaged the countryside in an orgy of spoliation and slaughter in the name of Revolution. In all its essentials Edward Farrell's appalling dream of that far-off night in Burgundy had come true.

By the time I myself reached young manhood in the middle years of our present century, the advent of railways had effectively put an end to the Grand Tour in its traditional form. It was, however, still a valued part of the education and formation of a gentleman to spend some time abroad in very much the same places as had been visited by the Greenwood travelling party in those years immediately prior to the

Revolution. Thus it was that I came to visit the site of what had once been the Château de Ménars. Given that Madame la Comtesse, whose evening readings to her daughters and to anyone else who cared to listen had enchanted those companionable gatherings, had been a Fairfax, I had felt something of an obligation to pay my respects, as it were. This was an unnerving experience. The shell of that homely chateâu was all that remained, abandoned and derelict; its roof had long since collapsed, windows and shutters were no more, the interior woodwork had long since disappeared, whether consumed by fire or pilfered for whatever purposes. One or two smoke-blackened fragments of wall were still standing, and there were piles of rubble overgrown with all manner of colourful wild plants where once there had been exquisite parquet, lovingly crafted and maintained. And from my Grandfather's diary entry I recalled then, as I do now, the warmth of the greetings and the happiness of the travellers' arrival at the Château in the autumn of 1785, the lovely, musical voices of the little girls, the torchlight on the steps against the night-time darkness of the surrounding forest, the rapidly re-established *camaraderie* of Sebastian and his cousins, Philippe and Aurélien, who died with their father, sword in hand, on the steps of that dear place in a futile attempt to protect their home and their beloved mother and little sisters, and who never did reach Warwickshire to hunt with Edward Farrell.

For me, as I stood contemplating those ruins of a fine if unpretentious house, the ruins of a cherished branch of my own family, it was as if a world had passed away, as indeed History informs us it did, in that year 1789 in France, when the old order of things was annihilated.

Disconsolate, I wandered briefly away from what had been the front of the Château and off into the rough grass where, some distance towards the beginnings of the forest fringes, my foot caught against something hard among the unkempt tufts of coarse herb and clods of untended earth, and I found myself gazing at the knobbly ball, unchanged no doubt by the passing of time or even the visitations of diabolic contingency. And at that point I allowed my sorrow to spill over into tears of bitter regret for those dear and precious lives so wantonly extinguished. I was briefly inclined to appropriate my find – for it had been very much a family affair, that silly medieval game, which had even survived the recent depredations of circumstance and human wickedness. But then I made the decision to leave it to lie where it properly belonged. And quite possibly it lies there still, before the ravaged remains of what was once the Château de Ménars.

For Edward Farrell, though, worse was to follow. By the time the news of such preliminary atrocities reached England, Edward had already taken up his commission in the Life Guards and was busily and enthusiastically caught up in the learning of his profession to be. His father, the fourth Earl, so disparagingly referred to by, among others, Mrs de Savigny, had assumed in his characteristic way that the son who returned to Warwickshire from his two years' absence abroad would be no different from the awkward, defiant young man who had been effectively abandoned to the interest and care of others. But there he was wrong. Edward was not that same young man and, mindful of advice from Mr Greenwood, he was easily able to engineer a confrontation with his parent in which the latter was disabused once for all of his slovenly assumptions. The young man managed, with some *finesse* and style, to make his point unequivocally.

"Father, I must beg you, sir, not to speak to me in that manner. It is not proper, not becoming to yourself, and above all, not gentlemanly."

"And do you presume, boy, to instruct *me* in what is gentlemanly? I shall whip you, by God!"

"No, sir. You will not."

What could it have been then, that the ageing Withybrook espied in his son's eyes to give him pause? Could there have been something, whatever it might have been, to compel the old man, however reluctantly, to acknowledge the more unpalatable truths of his own character? Certainly there had been no flicker of doubt, no wavering in the steady gaze which held his own so firmly. For Edward must have known that if he were to give way to his father on this first occasion, all the progress of the last two years would go by the board, and the intimidated, resentful, sullen boy would take him over again. It must have been quite simply a thought not to be contemplated. But he was now in a position to set the quiet style of Julian Greenwood against so distasteful a broil, a style accompanied by all the advice and wisdom he had imbibed from that gentleman of Lancashire over the many evenings of thoughtful conversation over their wine. And even as he knew that capitulation was out of the question, it distressed him to have to acknowledge what exactly his father was, even as he realised that the old man's complete lack of ordinary decency and civilised moral scruple did free him from his boyhood apprehensions.

Perhaps, then, something of his son's genuine contempt and the dismay which evidently accompanied it did convey itself to the father through the gaze, so unnervingly steady and unwavering, which the young man had fixed upon him? The contempt he must have seen certainly, for contempt is unmistakeable. Could he have inferred from that something of the distaste prompted by his own manner and style of utterance? Not to mention the genuine and concomitant disappointment in a young man who yearned to be able to love his father as a father should be loved but who found it impossible to do so? And there had been other things in those steady blue eyes. Edward had insisted he would not be whipped, and Lord Withybrook knew instinctively that this son would not capitulate to a father's authority unjustly exercised. Perhaps, also, there had been... pity? For one whose life had been thrown away upon trivia, one who had never acquired the *nous* to distinguish between what mattered and what did not? Lord Withybrook suddenly knew himself to be old, and privately he allowed that he had lost this particular clash of wills to an energetic young male avid for dominance. Edward would make a strong successor and, before that, a fine officer. Yes, by God! He should move up the Life Guards' hierarchy as fast as his father could buy him promotions, and the name of Withybrook, or Farrell at least, should *dazzle* in military circles.

"Oh very well, sir. But if..." Edward cut in, smiling at the petulant old man.

"No, sir. No but ifs... But now, sir, if I might suggest it, could we drink a bottle of the Condrieu I sent you together? It is a fine wine, Father. A fine French wine."

In this way a more amicable relationship was established between father and son, it happening too that the vain old earl's dreams of a rapid enhancement of the family standing through the swift purchase of military promotions did accord nicely with the son's purposes as well as with the drift of things where the development of events in across the Channel was concerned.

*

In the Autumn of 1793, with the Terror in that unhappy country at its height, Edward Farrell learned of the execution by guillotine of his privately beloved cousin, Clothilde de Châtigny – along with the rest of that family - in the public place in Paris. Prior to this, they had been torn from their quiet, elegant home in the Faubourg St Germain and incarcerated in the noisome dungeons of the Conciergerie, where they remained until it was their turn to be herded into tumbrels to be jolted through the stinking, demented, jeering streets to where the hellish machine, avid for yet more blood, awaited them. Those anxieties to which Gilbert de Châtigny had given voice to Julian Greenwood those several years previously had been made real in the worse possible manner. Edward Farrell was rendered helpless by the horror of what was implied in the way of anguish and despair beyond imagining, and when a compassionate Commanding Officer relieved him of immediate military duties he took refuge with his old friend, Sebastian Haverhill, now leading the life of a bachelor scholar in Hertfordshire.

This tragic episode in their lives is recorded in my Grandfather's journals of the time.

...Farrell arrived, unusually without warning, galloping like a madman into the peaceful seclusion of this modest estate. It was as though every devil in Hell were after him, and indeed he did bring with him the most dreadful news from France, for it seems that the Châtigny family are all murdered – to the very last of the little girls.

Farrell was quite beside himself; he had, it transpired, ridden the distance from London sobbing his heart out and shrieking out his rage and despair. And indeed I have never seen a man so profoundly discountenanced. The sight of his expression as he entered the house will remain with me for ever, as it no doubt will with the frightened little housemaid who announced, "The Captain, sir!" before fleeing back to the servants' quarters.

"May we be private?" Farrell asked, and I knew then, with a hideous foreboding, what it was he would have to say. We had of course known for a matter of years now about the wanton slaughter of the Ménars, and the destruction of the Chateau. And there had been horror enough in that, for to us – and to my Uncle Greenwood – it had been not only a loss of family, of cousins dearly loved, but an arbitrary, vile desecration of everything of value which we had cherished from that stage of our Tour – our strivings with the French language, the hunting with Philippe and Aurélien and Uncle Greenwood and Charles de Ménars, the family fun which Edward had learned to prize so dearly after his own solitary childhood, the silly old games in the 'coin des jeux du temps jadis', the exquisite readings by Madame la Comtesse of the old 'contes' in the evenings...Outside it was lovely, mellow morning; the colours of the foliage of the great trees around the house were at their most beautiful as they faded, prior to dropping.In my study Farrell turned to face me as I

followed him in, the tears pouring down cheeks still flushed from his headlong ride. He was barely able to utter a single word.

"Oh, Sebastian," he managed with huge effort, then choked helplessly as he sobbed.

"The Châtignys?" He nodded. "All of them?" He was unable to answer me, and I too found myself weeping without restraint as we clung to one another to lament the passing of what had been so precious and dear, and was now irrevocably gone. And just for an instant, the image of Ned, Philippe, Aurélien and myself as we might have been, in full career across Leicestershire fox country, imprinted itself upon my mind's eye; then it was gone. For ever.

"Do you imagine... that she... suffered?" he asked, and I realised then, effectively for the first time, how deeply and very privately he had cherished his tender feelings for the sweet cousin who had so graciously entertained his poor, early, stumbling efforts at her language.

"Anguish, yes," I said, finding it difficult actually to give voice to the thoughts that assaulted my mind like rough bullies tearing bestially at sweet decency. "violation we can only hope against hope that it was not so," and at this Ned tore himself away from me, turned his back and shrieked out his own grief and dismay, a tormented, despairing howl of utter desolation. It was as if the doors of Hell itself had opened just momentarily, in order that I might catch something of the cries of the damned within.

*

After this my Grandfather goes on to consider the situation of his old friend vis-à-vis the sweet lady whose life, along with the lives of her sisters, brothers and parents, had been so rudely curtailed, snuffed out, dismissed with contempt and hatred as of no more consequence than the noisome, bloody garbage of a butcher's shambles.

Edward Farrell must have known that, with his father still alive, there could never have been the slightest hope that he might be encouraged in his desire to pay his proper attentions to a foreign cousin who belonged to a Popish branch of the family. (And what a contrast here with the unassuming, happy accommodation of the Fairfax-Ménars connection.) Lord Withybrook, now ageing and enfeebled, may have capitulated - very likely not unwillingly, and even not without a degree of pride – to the young energy of Edward so urbanely exercised on his return from abroad. Given the established character of the old man, however, it seemed only too likely, on reflection, that he would have taken the opportunity to redress the balance against his son, to settle scores even in his approbation of what the boy was in process of becoming in his military career, for the slight implied in Edward's handling of their earlier clash. Lord Withybrook had never been a man to forgo the chance of bearing a grudge. So, Edward Farrell, intent on making a mark in his Army career, had cherished his deepest affections in the innermost privacy of his being. As a swordsman makes a particular point of defending the open line where he is most vulnerable to the possibility of an adversary's attack *in quarte,* so Edward had learned to remain on his guard where Clothilde de Châtigny was concerned. And although my Grandfather, his closest friend and *confidant,* had certainly been aware of his friend's feelings for his cousin at the time of their stay in Paris, Edward's reaction as the implications of the recent news from France autumn became clear to him, the first thoughts voiced in his grief:

"Do you imagine... she suffered?" spoke most eloquently to his old friend of the enduring character of his attachment. In due course of time Sebastian, content now in the bachelor existence of a gentleman scholar, wept bitterly within himself for the tragic misfortunes which had seemed with such malign

intent to have dogged his friend from his earliest days. For, however manfully and with whatever solid determination Edward Farrell had striven to become what Julian Greenwood had contrived to show him he could become, circumstances had rounded upon him yet again. And there were consequences to follow, for Farrell of the Life Guards was to become one of the most implacable hunters of Frenchmen it was possible to be. Throughout the nineties of the last century and on into the first decade of our own, throughout the Peninsula Campaign and finally right up to Waterloo itself, Edward Farrell killed Frenchmen with no more compunction than he would have had in killing any wild beast which threatened him and his own. Except that he had no own. Duly, my Grandfather was married to Miss Richards, and in 1805, the year in which Lord Nelson foiled the French at Trafalgar, my father, Edward, was born, the first of several Haverhills of that new generation, named quite naturally after a god-father who loved him to distraction and indulged the child quite ridiculously on those occasions when, free of military obligations, he was able to pay his visits.

In 1806 Edward Farrell became fifth Earl of Withybrook., by which time his sweet French cousin was already thirteen years dead and part of an era long gone. Some three years later Julian Greenwood also died, although happily not before he had witnessed the rise of his one-time protégé in the military service he rendered to his sovereign. For they had remained friends, my great, great Uncle Greenwood and Ned Farrell, with the latter often making the trip north to visit the old man in his Lancashire fastness, the modest manor up by the Forest of Bowland which now passed to a member of the Fairfax branch of the Greenwoods. Whether Julian had been aware of what it was that drove the ambitious young officer who had harnessed the black despair in his soul to the promotion of his military advancement, whether he and Sebastian ever discussed Edward Farrell one way or another I never did learn. But it must have seemed, with the death of Julian, almost as if the old century was in process of detaching itself from living memory in order to assume its new, diminished status as nothing more than the recollections of old journals, or the cautious words of scholars and antiquarians. For the past is no more than a matter of memory, in so far, that is, as it has any living reality; it becomes, as it were, a mere matter of prose crafted more or less responsibly, and with or without proper care.

There remained the business of the Corsican, Buonaparte, to be settled; the matter, to Edward Farrell now commanding his own regiment within the Brigade, of the ultimate quarry.

*

The history of the Emperor's eventual defeat and exile and his return to France over the Hundred Days of remission which followed is common knowledge, as is the story - so brilliantly recounted by Mr Thackeray – of the great ball at Brussels given by the Duchess of Richmond on the eve of Waterloo at which officers and their ladies danced and partied away the hours of night prior to the onset of hostilities.

Edward Farrell, fifth Earl of Withybrook, now commanding a brigade of cavalry, left the ball relatively early, to sit down with a last bottle in his quarters and compose a letter to his old friend, Sebastian Haverhill. I have that letter among my Grandfather's effects. It reads as follows:

My dear Sebastian – In a few hours now we shall be joining battle with the French, and I have it unequivocally from His Grace himself that it is his intention to make an end once and for all time to the activities of the French Emperor. I know also that Blücher and his Prussians are in total accord with this purpose, and hence surmise that the other commanders of the Alliance will be, too. Our world has suffered more than long enough from the vexatious antics of these French, and by God we have all given more than enough of our lifetimes in pursuit of them. However, one can never be certain what the outcome of such a day will turn out to be, for invariably in battle so much can and does depend and indeed hinge upon so little. You will therefore see this, I hope, as I intend it to be seen, as a provisional leave-taking and salutation to you and yours; especially, though, to you and to that fine young man, my namesake, who should in his turn go for a soldier and make a name for himself in honour of his military forebears in this, the finest of professions – if, of course, I may presume to advise a father upon his son's future. There is a provision in my will for your Edward, for there are obvious ways which I need not enumerate in which he has very much been the son I never did have. And indeed I do greatly regret having seen only so very little of him over his first years of life. There are also recommendations to the appropriate quarters within the Household Brigade, should you in due course judge it fitting that he follow me into the Guards. All of this is with the lawyers, who you know of, and is designed to serve its purpose at such a time as you may choose to have it do.

And now I shall not prolong this screed unduly. I must sleep an hour or two, and dawn will be breaking only too soon, to bring my good old John Hawkins with coffee and his, "Time to be up and about it, sir!" And how I have loved all that, the 'up and doing' aspects of the military existence. Truly, my career with the Brigade has been a kind of salvation for me, for whatever circumstances have made of me, without that I should have undoubtedly gone to rack and ruin in the style of that man, Peter de Savigny, who was married to your handsome aunt. And à propos, I understand that young Hawkhurst serves somewhere close by as an aide-de-camp today. May he weather the broil, as I myself hope to do, and come through unscathed by nightfall.

My dear Sebastian, may you prosper, you and your splendid family. My sense of what our friendship has been since Westminster days has quite simply never wavered,

*and I do sincerely trust that it, or the memory of it, will
endure in like manner in your recollections for as long as
you have yet to live.*

And now I must bid you au revoir, *and, God willing,* à
bientôt!

Ned

In the late afternoon of the battle Lord Withybrook was killed
instantly by a fragment of shrapnel from a gigantic shell-burst
directly over the heads of a group of commanders which
included the Duke of Wellington himself.

*

Thus, in terms of huge cost in lives and the prolonged misery
of years, the mad dog was neutered, the spectre that had been
the Revolution – which had escalated through Terror to
conquest in the name of republic then finally to a kind of
murderous, comic-opera empery – exorcised.

For my Grandfather the world changed irrevocably from
the moment that fragment of shell took away most of Ned
Farrell's head. Sebastian Haverhill sat alone in his study in
Hertfordshire and pondered the prospect of the new century
in the context of his old friend's last misfortune. And yet, he
mused, 'misfortune' was surely an ill-judged usage there. For
Ned had made his career in the Army and had been a successful
and highly regarded officer. The possibility of some such
contingency must have featured as a key element in his personal
equation. And besides, such a death – in the very thick of it all
– could hardly have been anything less than a desirable
consummation and not a thing any soldier would have shrunk
from. The contrast between that and the dreadful last moments
of the French cousins, and most probably from Ned's point of
view the agony of Clothilde de Châtigny, could hardly have
been more stark. Sebastian's one regret for his friend was
that Ned had not survived to know the outcome of the day

which, with the final eclipse of the dictator and his megalomaniac doings, would have seemed to have brought an era of unremitting conflict to a close.

Sebastian now looked forward in anticipation to a return to Germany, and a renewal of acquaintance with scholars and men of letters there, some of whom he had known since the time of his Tour all those years ago.

So in fact it was to be, for in the year following the final trial of conclusions at Waterloo Sebastian, on a brief excursion back to his beloved Germany, found himself in possession, almost by accident, of the newly published *German Legends* edited by the brothers Jacob and Wilhelm Grimm, with whom, over subsequent years, he was to sustain a lively correspondence. And indeed my Grandfather, in his later life, did visit the brothers, first at their home in Kassel, then in due course in Berlin, where no doubt the echoes of the merry voices of those vivacious young Steinberg ladies did not go unrecalled. Sebastian, of course, did also work himself on some of the earliest translations into the English language of what were to become known and famous as the Fairy Tales of the Brothers Grimm. And this it was that duly earned my Grandfather the approbation of our own German Prince Consort who sadly predeceased him by a matter of four years, the Prince dying of typhoid in 1861, Sebastian of extreme old age.

And amongst the Haverhill papers here in Hertfordshire from which I have compiled this narrative, there is one rather curious item, a piece written in the German language which has the appearance of a tale very much in the style of the Grimms, although it is quite clearly something more in the way of a close confidence for private recollection, a *quasi*-coded *aide-memoire* for a diary entry that, understandably, was never written. I have pondered long and hard as to whether it might properly be included among these reminiscences and have decided that, given the essentially private nature of this enterprise, and in view of the light it does throw on the captivating character of my Grandfather, it should be. I therefore reproduce it here in my own translation of the German original.

Es war einmal, vor langer Zeit, ein junger Herr... Once upon a time, a long time ago, a handsome young gentleman travelled the length and breadth of a fabulous land beyond the mountains. And with him there travelled also a sprightly and boon companion of many years' standing, a fine young nobleman destined in course of time to become a distinguished soldier and commander of armies which duly, in alliance with others of equal power, rid the world in timely fashion of a dreadful ogre whose evil forces had devastated their lands for many years. And with the two young men, the gentleman and his noble companion, there travelled also an elderly counsellor of great wisdom, one steeped in knowledge of the world abroad and of that magical place beyond the mountains, and familiar with the tongues of many lands. And as they made their way along highways, down rivers and over mountain passes, the young gentleman found that his thoughts would often return to the happy recollection of a handsome lady of rank and distinction who had once contrived to make it known to him, in the way such ladies have of doing these things, that his attentions would not be unwelcome, were he to favour her with them. And since the lady had been handsome, and full of spirit and mischief and merriment, the gentleman had responded to her intimations, so that together they had enjoyed an ecstasy of mutual rapture.

Imagine his delight, then, when it was made known to him by the wise counsellor that that same lady was to rendezvous with them on their return journey. This reunion was to take place at the fine residence of one of her many friends which was situated close by the homeward route they would be taking back up to the passes which led through the mountains.

The meeting did take place, and in the silence of the darkest hours of night the lady found her gentleman again, and they re-enacted their love for one another, and renewed the raptures of their earlier occasions. And as the dawn broke over the enchanted landscapes of that magical place - with its lakes and mountains, its gorgeous palaces, its castles dramatically, precariously perched on the brink of stupendous heights - the lady took leave of her gentleman and was swiftly gone from thence.

But in the course of time, in consequence of their embraces of that night, a fine son was born to the lady, one such as her depraved and monstrous husband could never have contrived to father upon her, even had he wished to do so, and even had she wished him to. And the boy grew to manhood, and entered into his noble inheritance, and became himself a leader and commander of men. And he successfully survived the many campaigns in which he played his part, and lived to a great age.

And the phrase from Ned Farrell's last letter to his old friend recurs to me now, as I sit here at this desk which was also my Grandfather's with the old papers spread out before me... *young Hawkhurst serves somewhere close by as an aide-de-camp today. May he weather the broil, as I myself hope to do, and come through unscathed by nightfall.* Could this have been Ned's prayer for the safe deliverance of his dear friend's other son, necessarily unacknowledged but no less discreetly loved for that? It does please me to think that it might have been, as it pleases me to be reminded that 'young Hawkhurst' lived a good, long life.